Marx
Abbott
Hardy
Defoe
Melville
Montaigne
Machiavelli
Chesterton
Cooper
Emerson
Haggard
Austen
Hugo
Eliot
Grimm
Stoker
Carroll
Christie
Maupassant
Byron
Molière
Schiller
Wilde
Garnett
Einstein
Fitzgerald
Hawthorne
Smith
Kafka
Goethe
Engels
Hall
Cotton
Kipling
Doyle
Willis
Baum
Henry
Dostoyevsky
Leslie
Dumas
Flaubert
Turgenev
Balzac
Stockton
Vatsyayana
Crane
Burroughs
Verne
Curtis
Tocqueville
Gogol
Vinci
Homer
Widger
Tolstoy
Whitman
Busch
Darwin
Thoreau
Twain
Potter
Freud
Zola
Lawrence
Scott
Plato
Harte
Kant
Jowett
Stevenson
Dickens
Burton
Hesse
Andersen
London
Descartes
Cervantes
Voltaire
Poe
Aristotle
Wells
Cooke
Hale
James
Hastings
Bunner
Shakespeare
Irving
Richter
Chambers
Doré
Dante
Swift
Chekhov
Shaw
da
Wodehouse
Benedict
Alcott
Pushkin
Newton

 tredition®

tredition was established in 2006 by Sandra Latusseck and Soenke Schulz. Based in Hamburg, Germany, tredition offers publishing solutions to authors and publishing houses, combined with world-wide distribution of printed and digital book content. tredition is uniquely positioned to enable authors and publishing houses to create books on their own terms and without conventional manufacturing risks.

For more information please visit: www.tredition.com

TREDITION CLASSICS

This book is part of the TREDITION CLASSICS series. The creators of this series are united by passion for literature and driven by the intention of making all public domain books available in printed format again - worldwide. Most TREDITION CLASSICS titles have been out of print and off the bookstore shelves for decades. At tredition we believe that a great book never goes out of style and that its value is eternal. Several mostly non-profit literature projects provide content to tredition. To support their good work, tredition donates a portion of the proceeds from each sold copy. As a reader of a TREDITION CLASSICS book, you support our mission to save many of the amazing works of world literature from oblivion. See all available books at www.tredition.com.

Project Gutenberg

The content for this book has been graciously provided by Project Gutenberg. Project Gutenberg is a non-profit organization founded by Michael Hart in 1971 at the University of Illinois. The mission of Project Gutenberg is simple: To encourage the creation and distribution of eBooks. Project Gutenberg is the first and largest collection of public domain eBooks.

Tales of Aztlan, the Romance of a Hero of our Late Spanish-American War, Incidents of Interest from the Life of a western Pioneer and Other Tales

George (Henry George August) Hartmann

Imprint

This book is part of TREDITION CLASSICS

Author: George (Henry George August) Hartmann
Cover design: Buchgut, Berlin – Germany

Publisher: tredition GmbH, Hamburg - Germany
ISBN: 978-3-8424-5520-7

www.tredition.com
www.tredition.de

Tales of Aztlan,

The Romance of a Hero of our Late Spanish-American War, Incidents of Interest from the Life of a western Pioneer and Other Tales

by

George Hartmann

A note about this book: A Maid of Yavapai, the final entry in this book, is dedicated to SMH. This refers to Sharlot M. Hall, a famous Arizona settler. The copy of the book that was used to make this etext is dedicated: With my compliments and a Happy Easter, Apr 5th 1942, To Miss Sharlot M. Hall, from The daughter of the Author, Carrie S. Allison, Presented March 31st, 1942, Prescott, Arizona.

1908 Revised edition

Memorial

That this volume may serve to keep forever fresh the memory of a hero, Captain William Owen O'Neill, U. S. V., is the fervent wish of The Author.

CONTENTS

CHAPTER I.

A FRAIL BARK, TOSSED ON LIFE'S TEM-PESTUOUS SEAS

A native of Germany, I came to the United States soon after the Civil War, a healthy, strong boy of fifteen years. My destination was a village on the Rio Grande, in New Mexico, where I had relatives. I was expected to arrive at Junction City, in the State of Kansas, on a day of June, 1867, and proceed on my journey with a train of freight wagons over the famous old Santa Fe trail.

Junction City was then the terminal point of a railway system which extended its track westward across the great American plains, over the virgin prairie, the native haunt of the buffalo and fleet-footed antelope, the iron horse trespassing on the hunting ground of the Arapahoe and Comanche Indian tribes. As a mercantile supply depot for New Mexico and Colorado, Junction City was the port from whence a numerous fleet of prairie schooners sailed, laden with the necessities and luxuries of an advancing civilization. But not every sailor reached his destined port, for many were they who were sent by the pirates of the plains over unknown trails, to the shores of the great Beyond, their scalpless bodies left on the prairie, a prey to vultures and coyotes.

If the plans of my relatives had developed according to program, this story would probably not have been told. Indians on the warpath attacked the wagon train which I was presumed to have joined, a short distance out from Junction City. They killed and scalped several teamsters and also a young German traveler; stampeded and drove off a number of mules and burned up several wagons. This was done while fording the Arkansas River, near Fort Dodge. I was delayed near Kansas City under circumstances which preclude the supposition of chance and indicate a subtle and Inexorably fatal power at work for the preservation of my life—a force which with the giant tread of the earthquake devastates countries and lays cities in ruins; that awful power which on wings of the cyclone slays the innocent babe in its cradle and harms not the villain, or vice versa; that inscrutable spirit which creates and lovingly shelters the sparrow over night and then at dawn hands it to the owl to serve him for his breakfast. Safe I was under the guidance of the same loving, paternal Providence which in death delivereth the innocent babe from evil and temptation, shields the little sparrow from all harm forever, and incidentally provides thereby for the hungry owl.

I should have changed cars at Kansas City, but being asleep at the critical time and overlooked by the conductor, I passed on to a station beyond the Missouri River. There the conductor aroused me and put me off the train without ceremony. I was forced to return, and reached the river without any mishap, as it was a beautiful moonlight night. I crossed the long bridge with anxiety, for it was a primitive-looking structure, built on piles, and I had to step from tie to tie, looking continually down at the swirling waters of the great, muddy river. As I realized the possibility of meeting a train, I crossed over it, running. At last I reached the opposite shore. It was nearly dawn now, and I walked to the only house in sight, a long, low building of logs and, being very tired, I sat down on the veranda and soon fell asleep. It was not long after sunrise that a sinister, evil-looking person, smelling vilely of rum, woke me up roughly and asked me what I did there. When he learned that I was traveling to New Mexico and had lost my way, he grew very polite and invited me into the house.

We entered a spacious hall, which served as a dining-room, where eight young ladies were busily engaged arranging tables and furniture. The man intimated that he kept a hotel and begged the young ladies to see to my comfort and bade me consider myself as being at home. The girls were surprised and delighted to meet me and overwhelmed me with questions. They expressed the greatest concern and interest when they learned that I was about to cross the plains.

"Poor little Dutchy," said one, "how could your mother send you out all alone into the cruel, wide world!" "Mercy, and among the Indians, too," said another. When I replied that my dear mother had sent me away because she loved me truly, as she knew that I had a better chance to prosper in the United States than in the Fatherland, they called me a cute little chap and smothered me with their kisses.

The tallest and sweetest of these girls (her name was Rose) pulled my ears teasingly and asked if her big, little man was not afraid of the Indians. "Not I, madame," I replied; "for my father charged me to be honest and loyal, brave and true, and fear not and prove myself a worthy scion of the noble House of Von Siebeneich." "Oh, my! Oh, my!" cried the young ladies, and "Did you ever!" and "No, I never!" and "Who would have thought it!" Regarding me wide-eyed with astonishment, they listened with bated breath as I explained that I was a lineal descendant of the Knight Hartmann von Siebeneich, who achieved everlasting fame through impersonating the Emperor Frederick (Barbarossa) of Germany, in order to prevent his capture by the enemy. I told how the commander of the Italian army, inspired with admiration by the desperate valor of the loyal knight, released him and did honor him greatly. And how this noble knight, my father's ancestor, followed the Emperor Frederick to the Holy Land and fought the Saracens. "And," added I, "my father's great book of heraldry contains the legend of the curse which fell on our house through the villainy of the Imperial Grand Chancellor of Blazonry, who was commanded to devise and procure a brand new heraldic escutcheon for our family.

"He blazoned our shield with the ominous motto, 'in der fix, Haben nix,' over gules d'or on a stony field, which was sown to a harvest of tares and oats, and embossed with a whirlwind rampant. As they were in knightly honor bound to live up to the motto on their shield, my ancestor were doomed to remain poor forever. At last they took service with the free city of Hamburg, where they settled finally and became honored citizens."

Happening to remember my mother's admonishment not to annoy people with too much talk, I apologized to the young ladies. Smilingly, they begged me to continue, for they seemed to enjoy my boyish prattle.

"Listen, now, girls," said Rose laughingly to her companions, "now, I shall make him open his mother's closet and show us her choicest family skeleton." "Oh, no, Miss Rose," I protested, "my mother has indeed a great closet, but it is full of good things to eat and contains no skeletons." "You little goosie-gander; you don't understand," replied Miss Rose; "I was only joking. Of course your mother kept the door carefully locked to keep you boys from foraging?" "No madame," said I, "it was not necessary to lock the door." "Did she keep a guard, then?" said Rose. "Oh, yes," I replied, "and it was very hard to pass in without being knocked down." "Was it a man?" she asked mischievously. "Why, yes; mamma kept a strong, old Limburger right behind the door," I said.

When the girls had ceased laughing, Rose said, "What did your mother tell you when you left for America?" "My mother," I answered, "implored me with tearful eyes to ever remember how my father's great-great-grandmother Brunhilde (who was exceedingly beautiful) was enticed into the depths of a dark forest by a wily, old German King. Indiscreetly and unsuspectingly she followed him. There clandestinely did he favor her graciously by adding a bar sinister to our knightly escutcheon and a strain of the blood royal to our family. This happened long, long ago in the dark ages or some other dark place—it may have been the Schwarzwald—and it was the curse of the stony field that did it.

"'Oh, my son,' mother urged me, 'we count on you to restore the unaccountably long-lost prestige of our ancient family. In America, behind the counters of your uncle's counting-rooms, you shall acquire great wealth, and his Majesty the Kaiser will be pleased to reinvest you with the coronet of a count. Then, as a noble count will you be of some account in the exclusive circle of the four hundred of the great city of New York. Beautiful heiresses will crave the favor of your acquaintance, and if wise, you will lead the most desirable one on the market, the lovely Miss Billiona Roque-a-Fellaire to the altar. His Majesty the Kaiser will then graciously change the "no-account" words on our family's escutcheon to the joyful motto, "Mit Geld," and lift the blighting curse from our noble house.'"

Next I related how surprised I was when I saw the great city of New York. However, I expected to see a large city of many houses, ever so high and some higher yet, and therefore I was not so very much surprised, after all. But in Illinois I first saw the wonderful forest. Oh, the virgin forest! Never had I seen such grand, beautiful trees, oak and hickory, ash and sycamore, maple, elm, and many more giant trees, unknown to me, and peopled by a multitude of wild birds of the brightest plumage. There were birds and squirrels everywhere! I actually saw a sky-blue bird with a topknot, and another of a bright scarlet color, and gorgeous woodpeckers who were too busy hammering to look at me even. Oh, but they did not sing like the birds in Germany! All were very grave and sad. They seemed to know, as everybody else did, that I was a stranger in their land, for they gave me all sorts of useful Information and advice, with many nods of their little heads.

"Peep, peep!" counseled the bluebird. "Thank you," I replied, "seeing is believing." "Whip-poor-will, whip-poor-will," cried a large, spotted bird. "That," thought I, "is a prize fighter." "Cheat, cheat!" urged a pious-looking cardinal, who evidently mistook me for a gambler. "Don't," roared a bullfrog, who was seated on a log and winked his eye at me. "There is an honest man," I thought. "Shake, good sir." In consternation and surprise, I instantly released his hand. "HOW is it possible to be both honest and slippery at the same time! This must be a Yankee-man," thought I. I saw real moss, green and velvety as the richest carpet, and I drank of singing, bubbling waters. Many kinds of berries and nuts, hard to crack, grew in the wild glens of the forest. I gathered flowers, larger and more beautiful than any I had ever seen, but they lacked the perfume of German flowers; only the roses were the same.

Many children did I see, but they had not the rosy cheeks of German children. And I met the strongest of all beasts on earth and tracked him to his native lair; and there, in the sacred groves of the Illini, I worried him sorely, and as David did unto Goliath, so did I unto him; and sundown come, I slew him. And for three-score days and ten the smoke of battle scented the balmy air.

The young ladles laughed heartily and said that never before had they been so delightfully entertained, and they gave me sweets and nice things to eat, and said they hoped I might stay with them forever and a day. We exchanged confidences, and they warned me to beware of the landlord, who had been known to rob people. They advised me to secrete my money, if perchance I had any. I thanked them kindly, replying that I had only one dollar in my purse. This was true, but I did not tell them that I had sewed a large sum in banknotes and some German silver into my kite's tail when I set out on my journey to the West.

I complimented these charming girls on their good fortune to be in the service of so generous a gentleman as their landlord seemed to be; for I saw that they wore very fine dresses and had many jewels. "Why, you little greenie," said Miss Rose, "he does not pay us high wages." "Oh, I see, how romantic! how nice!" exclaimed I. "You do as the ladies in the good old time of chivalry, when knights donned their colors and sallied forth to battle with lions and tigers. You crave largesse, and the gentlemen favor you with money and jewels." Then the youngest girl laughed and said, "Oh, you pore, innicent bairn, and how do yez ken all this? and how did yez know that Misther Payterson kapes a tiger at all, at all, begorra!" Another young lady said, "Dutchy, I reckon yore daddy is a right smart cunning old fox!" "Madame," replied I, indignantly, "my father is no fox, but a minister of the Gospel." "Oh, this bye is the son of a praste," screamed the loveliest girl in all Missouri. "Indade, I misthrusted the little scamp. Och! oh and where is me brooch? I thought all the time the little divvil was afther something. Thieves! Murther!" Confusion in pandemonium now reigned supreme. For one precious moment the air seemed full of long-legged stockings and delicate hands and purses. Luckily, the brooch was found and peace restored at once. And Rose said, "Oh, girls, how could you!" and she begged my pardon and said they did not mean it. And then I made myself very useful and agreeable to these lovely maids, lacing their shoes and dusting their chamber, and right gallantly did I serve them until evening.

After supper reappeared my evil genius in the person of the landlord, who took me out to the woodshed. "Dutchy, I have decided to adopt you as my only son; have you ever bucked a wood saw?" said he, and a sardonic leer distorted his evil features. After I recovered sufficiently from the shock, I answered indignantly, "Sir, know ye not that I have pledged my service to the vestal virgins of yon temple?" "Ha! Ha!" laughed the villain, "get busy now, son, and if by morning this wood has not been cut, you will go minus your breakfast." Thereupon he locked me in.

Caught as a rat in a trap, I had no alternative but to comply with this man's outrageous demands. Despairingly I plied that abominable instrument of torture, the national bucksaw of America. This is the only American institution I could never accustom myself to. I have endured bucking bronchos in New Mexico, I have bucked the tiger in Arizona, but to buck a wood-saw—perish the thought! Sore and weary, I lay down in a corner of the shed on some hay and fell asleep. I dreamed that I heard screams of women, mingled with song and laughter, and through it all the noise of music and dancing. Then the dream changed into a horrible nightmare in the shape of a big sawhorse which kicked at me and threatened me with hard labor.

Toward morning, when the door was opened and a drunken ruffian entered, I awoke from my troubled slumbers. "Hi, Dutchy, and have yez any tin?" he threatened. "Kind sir," I replied, "when I departed for the West I left all my wealth behind me." Verily, now I was proving myself the worthy scion of valiant men, who had laid aside hauberk, sword, and lance, taken up the Bible and stole, and thenceforth fought only with the weapon of Samson, the strong!

"And so yez are, by special appointment, chamberlain to the gurruls by day, and ivver sawing wood at nighttime! Bedad! I'll shpile the thrick for Misther Payterson, the thaving baste, and take this little greenhorn out of his clutches and sind him about his business." With these words, he opened the door for me and I escaped.

Farewell, lovely maids of Kansas and Missouri! If mayhap this writing comes to you, oh, let us meet again; my heart yearns to greet you and your granddaughters. For surely, though it seems to me as yesterday, the blossoms of forty summers have fallen in our path and whitened our hair.

CHAPTER II.

PERILOUS JOURNEY

After several days I arrived at the end of my railway journey, Junction City, without delay or accident. The trip was not lacking in interesting details. The monotony of the never ending prairie was at times enlivened by herds of buffalo and antelope. On one occasion they delayed our train for several hours. An enormous herd of thousands upon thousands of buffalo crossed the railroad track in front of our train. Bellowing, crowding, and pushing, they were not unlike the billows of an angry sea as it crashes and foams over the submerged rocks of a dangerous coast. Their rear guard was made up of wolves, large and small. They followed the herd stealthily, taking advantage of every hillock and tuft of buffalo grass to hide themselves. The gray wolf or lobo, larger and heavier than any dog, and adorned with a bushy tall was a fierce-looking animal, to be sure. The smaller ones were called coyotes or prairie wolves, and are larger than foxes and of a gray-brown color. These are the scavengers of the plains, and divide their prey with the vultures of the air.

At times we passed through villages of the prairie dog, consisting of numberless little mounds, with their owners sitting erect on top. When alarmed, they would yelp and dive into their lairs in the earth. These little rodents share their habitations with a funny-looking little owl and the rattlesnake. I believe, however, that the snake is not there as a welcome visitor, but comes in the role of a self-appointed assessor and tax gatherer. I picked up and adopted a little bulldog which had been either abandoned on the cars or lost by its owner, not then thinking that this little Cerberus, as I called it, should later prove, on one occasion, to be my true and only friend when I was in dire distress and in the extremity of peril.

The town of Junction City, which numbered less than a score of buildings and tents, was in a turmoil of excitement, resembling a nest of disturbed hornets. Several hundred angry-looking men crowded the only street, every one armed to the teeth. The great majority were dark-skinned Mexicans, but here and there I noticed the American frontiersman, the professional buffalo hunter and scout. These were men of proved courage, and I observed that the Mexicans avoided looking them squarely In the face; and when meeting on the public thoroughfare, they invariably gave them precedence of passage.

I found opportunity to hire out to a pleasant-looking young Mexican as driver of a little two-mule provision wagon. In this manner I earned my passage across the plains. Don Jose Lopez, that was his name, said that I need not do much actual work, as he would have his peons attend to the care of the mules and have them harness up as well. He also told me that we would have to delay our departure until every team present in the town had its cumulation of cargo. They dared not travel singly, he said, for the Indians were very hostile. In consequence whereof our departure was delayed for six weeks. I camped with the Mexicans and accustomed myself very soon to their mode of living. The fact that I understood their language and spoke it quite well was a never-ending surprise and mystery to them. I took dally walks over the prairie to the junction of two creeks, a short distance from the town, bathed and whiled away the time with target practice, and soon became very proficient in the use of firearms.

The banks of these little streams would have made a delightful picnic ground, covered as they were by a luxuriant growth of grasses and bushes and some large trees also, mostly of the cottonwood variety. But there were no families of ladies and children here to enjoy the lovely spot. A feeling of intense uneasiness seemed to pervade the very air and a weird presentiment of impending horror covered the prairie as with a ghostly shroud. The specter of a wronged, persecuted race ever haunted the white man's conscience. In vain did the red man breast the rising tide of civilization. In their sacred tepees, their medicine men invoked the aid of their great Spirit and they were answered.

The Spirit sent them for an ally, an army of grasshoppers, which darkened the sun by its countless numbers. It impeded the progress of the iron horse, but not for long. Then he sent them continued drouth, but the pale face heeded not. "Onward, westward ever, the star of empire took its course."

We camped out on the prairie within a short distance and in full sight of the town. I made the acquaintance of a merchant, Mr. Samuel Dreifuss, who kept a little store of general merchandise. This gentleman liked to converse with me in the German tongue and was very kind to me, even offering to employ me at a liberal salary, which I, of course, thankfully declined. One morning after breakfast I went to this store to purchase an article of apparel. The door was unlocked and I entered, but found no one present. I waited a while, and as Mr. Dreifuss did not appear, I knocked at the bedroom door, which was connected with the store. Receiving no response to my knocks, I opened the door and entered. There was poor Mr. Dreifuss lying stone dead on his couch. I knew that he was dead, for his hands were cold and clammy to the touch. I was struck with astonishment. The day before had I spoken to him, when he appeared to be hale and hearty. There were some ugly, black spots on his face, and I thought that it was very queer. I did not see any marks of violence on his person and nothing unusual about the premises. I looked around carefully, as a boy is apt to do when something puzzles him. Then I thought I would go up-town and tell about this strange circumstance.

The store was the first building met with in the town if a person came from the railway station. As I went toward the next house, which was a short distance away, I was hailed by a tall, broad-shouldered man with long hair, who commanded me to halt. I kept right on, however, meaning to tell him about my gruesome discovery. As I advanced toward him he retreated, and I called to him to have no fear, as I did not intend to shoot. The big man shook with laughter and cried, "Hold, boy, stop there a minute until I tell you something. They say that 'Wild Bill' never feared man, but I fear you, a mere boy. Did you come out of that store?" "Yes, sir," I said. "And did you see the Jew?" "Yes, sir," I answered; "Mr. Dreifuss is dead." "How do you know that?" he questioned. "His hands feel cold as ice," I said, "and there is a black spot on his nose." Again the man laughed and said, "Do you know what killed him?" "I do not know, sir," I answered, "but I was going uptown to inquire." "Well," said the scout, "Mr. Dreifuss had the cholera." "That's too bad," said

I; "let us go back and see if we can be of any assistance." "No, you don't," said the long-haired scout; "I have been stationed here, as marshal of the town, to warn people away from the place. You take my advice and go to the creek and plunge in with all your clothes and play for an hour in the water, then dry yourself, go back to camp, and keep mum!" This was the year of the cholera. It started somewhere down south, and many people died from it in the city of St. Louis, and it followed the railway through Kansas to the end of the track. Many soldiers died also at Fort Harker, which was farther out West on the plains.

At last we started on our perilous journey, an imposing caravan of one hundred and eighty wagons, each drawn by five yoke of oxen. Our force numbered upward of two hundred and fifty men, the owners, teamsters, train masters or mayordomos and the herders of the different outfits; all were Mexicans except myself.

Several days were spent in crossing the little stream formed by the confluence of two creeks. The water was quite deep and had to be crossed by means of a ferryboat. Here I met with my first adventure, which nearly cost me my life. My wagon was loaded with supplies and provisions and with several pieces of oak timber, intended for use in our train. When I drove down the steep bank on to the ferryboat, the timbers, which were not well secured, slid forward and pushed me off my seat, so that I fell right under the mules just as they stepped on the ferry. The frightened mules trampled and kicked fearfully. I lay still, thinking that if I moved they would step on me, as their hoofs missed my head by inches only. I thought of my mother and how sorry she would be if she could see me now, but I was thinking, ever thinking and lay very still. Then my guardian angel, in the person of a Mexican, crawled under the wagon from the rear end and pulled me by my heels, back to safety under the wagon. When I came out from under I threw my hat in the air and gave a whoop and cheer, at which the Mexicans were greatly enthused. They yelled excitedly and our mayordomo exclaimed: "Caramba, mira que diablito!" (Egad, see the little devil!)

We traveled in two parallel lines, about fifty feet apart and kept the spare cattle and remounts of horses, as also the small provision teams between the lines. A cavalcade of train owners and mayordomos was constantly scouting in all directions, but they never ventured out of sight of the traveling teams. We started daily at sunrise and traveled till noon or until we made the distance to our next watering place. Then we camped and turned our live stock out to rest and crop the prairie grass. After several hours we used to resume our journey until nightfall or later to our next camping ground. Every man had to take his turn about at herding cattle and horses during the nighttime. Only the cooks were exempt from doing herd and guard duty.

We pitched our nightly camps by forming two closed half circles of our wagons, one on each side of the road so as to form a corral. By means of connecting the wagons with chains, this made a strong barricade, quite efficient to repulse the attacks of hostile Indians, if defended by determined men. Every freight train when in camp was a little fort in itself and an interesting sight at nighttime, when the blazing fires were surrounded by men who were cooking and passing the time in various ways. Some were cleaning and loading their guns, others mended their clothes. Here and there you would find some genius playing dreamy, monotonous Spanish airs on the guitar, in the midst of a merry group of dancing and singing young Mexicans, many of whom were not older than I. Card-playing seemed, however, to be their favorite pastime; all Mexicans are inveterate gamesters, who look upon the profession of gambling as an honorable and desirable occupation.

After the first day out I did not see an inebriated man in the whole party. The Mexicans are really a much maligned and slandered people. They are often charged with the sin of postponing every imaginable thing until manana, but, to do them justice, I must say that they drank every drop of liquor they carried on the first day out; also ate all the dainties which other people would have saved and relished for days to come. Surely, not manana, but ahora, or "do it now" was their soul-stirring battle cry on this occasion.

After several days of travel we encountered herds of buffalo and mustangs or wild horses, and when our scouts reported numerous Indian signs, we advanced slowly and carefully, momentarily expecting an ambuscade and attack. Our column halted frequently

while our horsemen explored suspicious-looking hillocks and ra-
vines.

A dense column of smoke rose suddenly in our front, and I saw
several detachments of Indian warriors on a little hill, who were
evidently reconnoitering, and spying our strength, but did not expose themselves fully to view. Simultaneously columns of signal
smoke arose in all directions round about. Instantly our lines closed
in the front and rear and we came to an abrupt halt. What I saw
then made my heart sink, for the drivers seemed to be paralyzed
with terror. The very men who had heretofore found a great delight
in trying to frighten me with tales of Indian atrocities were now
themselves scared out of their wits. Young and inexperienced
though I was, I realized that to be now attacked by Indians meant to
be slaughtered and scalped. Some of the men were actually crying
from fright, seeming to be completely demoralized. I noticed how
one of our men in loading his musket rammed home a slug of lead,
forgetting his charge of powder entirely. The sight of this disgusted
me so that I became furious, and in the measure that my anger rose
my fear subsided and vanished. I railed at the poor fellow and
abused and cursed him shamefully, threatening to kill him for being
a coward and a fool. I made him draw the bullet and reload his
musket in a proper manner.

When I grew older I acquired the faculty to curb the instinctive
feeling of fear which is inborn in all creatures and undoubtedly is a
wise provision of nature, necessary to the continuance of life and
conducive to self-preservation. Knowing that all men who ever
lived and all who now live must surely die, I failed to see anything
particularly fearful in death. I may truthfully say that I have several
times met death face to face squarely and feared not. On these occa-
sions I tried not to escape what seemed to be my final doom, but in
the dim consciousness of mind that I should be dead long enough
anyway, I tried to delay my departure to a better life as long as possible, exerting myself exceedingly to accomplish this purpose. Undoubtedly this must have made me a very undesirable person to
contend with in a fight. Luckily for me, I have never been afflicted
with a quarrelsome or vindictive mind. This is not a boastful or
frivolous assertion, but is uttered in the spirit of thankfulness to the
allwise Creator of Heaven and earth.

Looking around, I beheld a sight which cheered me mightily. There, a few yards ahead of my wagon, was a great hole in the ground, made by badgers; or it may have been the palace of a king of prairie dogs. Quickly I drove my team forward, right over it. Then, pretending to be rearranging my cargo, I took out the end gate of my wagon and covered the hole with it. Next, I wet some gunny sacks and placed them on the ground under the board. Now, thought I, here is my chance for an honorable retreat if anything should go wrong. I intended to close up the hole behind me with the wet sacks, taking the risk of snake bites in preference to the tender mercies of the Indians. As these ground lairs take a turn a few feet down and are connected with various underground passages and have several outlets, I had a fair prospect to escape should the Indians discover my whereabouts, for they could neither burn nor smoke me out, and were not likely to take the time to reduce my fort by starvation. It took me but a very short time to make my preparations, and I did it unnoticed by my companions, who seemed fully preoccupied with their own troubles.

A horseman galloped up to our division, a great, swarthy, fierce-looking man, bearded like the pard. This man did not act like a scared person. One glance at the frightened faces of his countrymen sufficed to enlighten and also to enrage him.

"Senores," he said, "I perceive you are anxious and ready for a fight. I hope the Indians will accommodate us, as we are greatly in need of a little sport. It may happen that some of you will lose your scalps, and I hope that it is not you, Senor Felipe Morales. I should be very sorry for your poor old mother and your crippled sister, for who will support them if you should fail them? As for you, Senor Juan, it does not matter much if you never again breathe the air of New Mexico. Your young little wife has not yet had an opportunity to know you fully, anyway, and your cousin, the strapping Don Isidro Chavez, will surely take the best care of her. They say he calls on her daily to inquire after her welfare. Senor Cuzco Gonzales, as you might be unlucky enough to leave your bones on this prairie, I would advise you to make me heir to your garden of chile peppers. To be sure, I never saw a more tempting crop! Mayhap you will have no further use for chile, as the Indians are likely to heat your belly with hot coals, in lieu of peppers."

Then he called for the cook. "Senor Doctor," he said, "prepare the medicine for this man, who is too sick to load a musket properly, and had to be shown how to do so by a little gringo, as I observed a while ago. Hold him, Senores." And they held him down while the cook administered the medicine, forcing it down his unwilling throat. The medicine was compounded from salt, and the prescribed dose was a handful of it dissolved in a tin cupful of water. This seemed to revive the patient's faltering spirit wonderfully. The cook, a half-witted fellow, was another man who seemed to have no fear. His eyes shone wickedly and he was stripped for the fight. A red bandanna kerchief tied around his head, he glided stealthily about, thirsty for Indian blood as any wolf. They told me that his mother and sister had died at the hands of the cruel Apaches.

To me the rider said, "Senor Americanito, I know your gun is loaded right and is ready to shoot straight. Look you, if you plant a bullet just below an Indian's navel, you will see him do a double somersault, which is more wonderful to behold than any circus performance you ever saw."

Here was a man good to see, a descendant of the famous Don Fernando Cortez, conquistador, and molded on the lines of Pizarro, the wily conqueror of Peru, and he heartened our crew amazingly. He exhorted the men to be brave and fight like Spaniards, and he prayed to the saints to preserve us; and piously remembering his enemies, he called on the devil to preserve the Indians. Such zealous devotion found merited favor with the blessed saints in Heaven, for they granted his prayer, and the Indians did not attack us that day.

On the following day, Don Emillo Cortez came again and asked me to ride with him as a scout. He had brought a young man to drive the team in my stead. Gladly I accepted his invitation. He arranged a pillion for his saddle and mounted me behind him, facing the horse's tail. Then he passed a broad strap around his waist and my body and armed me with a Henry repeating rifle, then a new invention and a very serviceable gun. In this manner I had both hands free and made him the best sort of a rear guard. We cantered toward a sandy hill on our left. A coyote came our way, appearing from the crest of the hill. The animal was looking back over its shoulder and veered off when it scented us. Don Emilio halted his horse. "That coyote is driven by Indians," said he; "do you think you can hit it at this distance?" I thought I could by aiming high and a little forward. At the crack of my rifle the coyote yelped and bit its side, then rolling on the grass, expired. "Carajo! a dead shot, for Dios!" exclaimed Don Emilio. "That will teach the heathen Indians to keep their distance; they will not be over-anxious to meet these two Christians at close quarters!"

We were not molested on this day nor on the next, but on the day thereafter we were in terrible danger. The Indians fired the dry grass, and if the wind had been stronger we must have been burned to death. As it was we were nearly suffocated from traveling in a dense smoke for several hours. Then, fortunately, we reached the bottom lands of the Arkansas River and were safe from fire, as the valley was very wide and covered with tall green grass which could not burn; and no sooner was the last wagon on safe ground than the fire gained the rim of the green bottomland. Our oxen were exhausted and in a bad plight, so we fortified and camped here for several days to recuperate before we forded the river. This took up several days, as the water was quite high and the river bottom a dangerous quicksand. To stop the wheels of a wagon for one moment meant the loss of the wagon and the lives of the cattle, perhaps. The treacherous sands would have engulfed them. Forty yoke of oxen were hitched to every vehicle, and we had no losses. On the other side we found the prairie burned over, and we traveled all day until evening in order to reach a suitable camping place with sufficient grass for our animals. As there was no water and the cattle were suffering, we were compelled to drive our herd back to the river and return again that same night. The rising sun found us under way again, and by noon we came to good camping ground with an abundance of grass and water.

CHAPTER III.

THE MYSTERY OF THE SMOKING RUIN. STALKING A WARRIOR. THE AMBUSH

Now we were past the most dangerous part of our journey, leaving the Comanche country and entering the domain of the Ute Indians and other tribes, who were not as brave as the Arapahoes and Comanches. Here our caravan-formation was broken up and each outfit traveled separately at its own risk.

The next day we witnessed a most horrible and distressing sight. Willingly would I surrender several years of my allotted lifetime on earth if I could thereby efface forever the awful impression of this pitiful tragedy from my memory. Alas I that I was fated to behold the shocking sight! For days thereafter we plodded on, a sad-looking, sober, downhearted lot of men, grieved to distraction, and there I left the innocence of boyhood—wiser surely, but not better! We neared the still smoking ruins of what had once been a happy home. As I approached to gratify my curiosity, I met several of my companions, who were returning and who implored me not to go nearer. An old Mexican, ignorant, rough, and callous as he was, begged me, with tears streaming down his face, to retrace my steps. Alas, when would impulsive youth ever listen to wise counsel and take heed! I entered the ruins and saw a dark telltale pool oozing forth from under the door of a cellar. Oh, had I but then overcome my morbid curiosity and fled! But no! I must needs open the door and look in. I saw—I saw a beautiful whiskey barrel, its belly bursted and its head stove in!

The trip across the plains was a very healthful and pleasant experience to me. During the greatest heat and while the moon favored us, we often traveled at night and rested in daytime. By foregoing my rest, I found opportunity to hunt antelope and smaller game. I was very fond of this sport and indulged in it frequently. One day I sighted a band of antelope—these most beautiful and graceful animals. I tried to head them off, in order to get within rifle-shot distance, and drifted farther and farther away from camp until I must have strayed at least five miles. Like a rebounding rubber ball, their four feet striking the ground simultaneously, they fled until at last they faded from sight on the horizon, engulfed in a shimmering wave of heat, the reflection from a sun-scorched ground. Reluctantly I gave up the chase, as I could by no means approach the game, although they could not have winded me.

In order to determine the direction of our camp, I ascended a little hill, when I suddenly espied an Indian. He was in a sitting posture, less than a quarter of a mile away. Apparently he was stark naked and his face was turned away from me, for I saw his broad back where not covered by his long hair glisten in the hot rays of the sun. His gun was lying within reach of his right hand, but I could not see what he was doing. On the impulse of the moment I dropped behind a flowering cactus for concealment. Then I took counsel with myself and decided that it would be too risky to return to camp as I had intended to do. In that direction for a long distance the ground was gently rising and most likely the Indian would have seen me. I thought it probable that he had staked his horse out in some nearby gulch, and if seen I would have been at his mercy, as perhaps he was also in touch with other Indians of his tribe. I reasoned that I could not afford to make the mistake of incurring the risk to stake my life on the chance of escaping his observation. I had started out to hunt antelopes, but now I coolly prepared myself to stalk an Indian warrior instead. I went about it as if I were hunting a coyote. First of all, I ascertained the direction of the wind, which was very light. It blew from the quarter the Indian was in toward me. Next, lying on my stomach, I dug the large flowering plant up, and holding it by its roots in front of myself, I crawled toward my quarry, as a snake in the grass. Cautiously, stealthily, avoiding the slightest noise, and always on the lookout for snakes and thorns, I crept slowly on, making frequent halts to rest myself. Twice the Indian turned his head and looked in my direction, but apparently he did not perceive me. In this manner I came within easy gunshot distance. Now I took my last rest, and with my knife dug a hole in the ground and replanted my cactus shield firmly. Then I placed my rifle in position to fire and drew a fine bead on the nape of his neck.

"Adios, Indian brave, prepare thy soul to meet the great Spirit in the ever grassy meadows of the happy hunting grounds of eternity, for the spider of thy fate is weaving the last thread in the web of thy doom!" My finger was coaxing the trigger, when a feeling of intense shame rose fiercely in my breast. Was I, then, like unto this Indian, to take an enemy's life from ambush? Up I jumped with a challenging shout, my gun leveled, ready for the fight. "Por Dios, amigo, amigo!" cried the frightened Indian, holding up his hands. "No tengo dinero!" (I have no money. Don't shoot!) he begged, speaking to me in Spanish. Then I went to him and learned that he belonged to a wagon train, traveling just ahead of us. He was a full-blood Navajo, who had been made captive in a Mexican raid into the Navajo country. The Mexicans used to capture many Navajo pappooses and bring them up as bond servants or peons. This Indian told me that he had been following the same band of antelopes as myself, and on passing a beautiful hill of red ants, he yielded to temptation and thought he would have his clothes examined and laundered by the ants. These little insects are really very accommodating and work without remuneration. At the same time he likewise took a sun bath on the same liberal terms. This episode made me famous with every Spanish freighter over the Santa Fe trail, from Kansas into New Mexico.

Just before we reached the Cimarron country, which is very hilly and is drained by the Red River, and where we were out of all danger from Indians, I had a narrow escape from death. I was in the lead of our train and had crossed a muddy place in the road. I drove on without noticing that I was leaving the other teams far behind. A wagon stuck fast in the mire, which caused my companions a great deal of labor and much delay. At last I halted to await the coming of the other teams. Suddenly there fell a shot from the dense growth of a wild sunflower copse. It missed my head by a very close margin and just grazed the ear of one of the mules. I believe that if I had attempted to rejoin the train then I would have been killed from ambush. Instead, I quickly secured the brake of my wagon, then I unhooked the trace chains of the mules and quieted them and lay down under the wagon, ready to defend myself. I was, however, not further molested and my companions came along after a while. They had heard the shot and thought it was I who had fired it.

CHAPTER IV.

A STRANGE LAND AND STRANGER PEO-PLE

We were now within the boundaries of the Territory of Colorado and approaching the northern line of New Mexico. When we passed through Trinidad, which was then a small adobe town, we met Don Emilio Cortez again. He was at home in this vicinity and came for the express purpose of persuading me to come with him. "My good wife charged me to bring her that little gringo," he said; "she longs for an American son." "Our daughter, Mariquita, is now ten years of age, and has been asked in marriage by Don Robusto Pesado, a very rich man. But the child is afraid of him, as he is a mountain of flesh, weighing close on twelve arrobas. Now we thought that two years hence thou wilt be seventeen years old and a man very sufficient for our little Mariquita, who will then, with God's favor, be a woman of twelve years. She will have a large dowry of cattle and sheep, and as the saints have blessed us with an abundance of land and chattels, thou art not required to provide."

I thanked Don Emilio very kindly, but was, of course, too young then to entertain any thought of marrying. I was really sorry to disappoint him, as he seemed to have formed a genuine attachment for me and was seriously grieved by my refusal.

Rumor spreads its vagaries faster among illiterate people than among the enlightened and educated. Therefore, it was said in New Mexico long before our arrival there that Don Jose Lopez's outfit brought a young American, the like of whom had never been known before. He was not ignorant, as other Americans, for he not only spoke the Spanish, but he could also read and write the Castillan language. It was well known that most Americans were so stupid that they could not talk as well as a Mexican baby of two years, and that often after years of residence among Spanish people they were still ignorant of the language. And would you believe it, but it was the sacred truth, this little American, albeit a mere boy, had the strength of a man. He made that big heathen Navajo brute

Pancho, the mayordomo of Don Preciliano Chavez, of Las Vegas, stand stark before him in his nakedness, with his hands raised to Heaven and compelled him, under pain of instant death, to say his Pater Noster and three Ave Marias. Others said that Don Jose Lopez was a man of foresight and discretion and saw that the Indians were on the warpath and very dangerous. Therefore, he prayed to his patron saint for spiritual guidance and succor. San Miguel, in his wisdom, sent this young American heretic, as undoubtedly it was best to fight evil with evil. And when the devil, in the guise of a coyote, led the Indians to the attack, then he was sorely wounded by the unerring aim of the gringito's rifle.

Others said that Don Jose Lopez had set up a shrine for the image of his renowned patron saint, San Miguel, in his provision wagon, which was being driven by the American boy, and the boy took the bullet which wounded the coyote so sorely out of the saint's mouth, who had bitten the sign of the cross thereon. And the evil one, in the likeness of the coyote, rolled in his agony on the grass when he was hit by the cross-marked bullet. Of course, the grass took fire and very nearly burned up the whole caravan.

Other people said they were not surprised to hear of miracles emanating from the shrine of the patron saint of Don Jose. His grandfather had whittled this famous image out of a cottonwood tree, whereon a saintly Penitente had been crucified after the custom of the order of Flagellants. This Penitente resembled the penitent thief who died on the cross and entered Paradise with the Saviour in this, that he was known to be a good horse thief, and as he had died on the cross on a night of Good Friday, he surely went to Glory Everlasting. Don Jose's grandfather made a pilgrimage with this image he had made to the City of Mexico, to have the Archbishop bless it in the cathedral before Santa Guadalupe. During the ceremony, it was said, there grew a fine head of flaxen hair on the image and it received beautiful blue eyes. And it had the miraculous propensity to ever after wink its eye in the presence of a priest and at the approach of a Christ-hating Jew, it would spit. This virtue saved much wealth for the family of Don Jose, as they were ever put on their guard against Jewish peddlers.

The rumor that Don Jose Lopez had carried the household saint with him in his wagon was at once contradicted and disproved by his wife, Dona Mercedes. The lady declared that San Miguel had never left his shrine in the patio of their residence except for the avowed purpose of making rain. In seasons of protracted drouth, when crops and live stock suffer for want of water, crowds of Mexican people, mostly farmers' wives and their children, form processions and carry the images of saints round about the parched fields, chanting hymns and praying for rain.

On this occasion Dona Mercedes availed herself of the chance to extol the prowess and power of her family's idolized saint, San Miguel. She said as a rainmaker he had no equal. He disliked and objected to have himself carried about the fields when there was not a certain sign of coming rain in the heavens. Her little saint, she said, was too honorable and too proud to risk the disgrace of failure and bring shame on her family. Therefore, he would not consent to be carried out in the fields until kind Nature, through unfailing signs, proclaimed a speedy downpour. When thunder shook the expectant earth and the first drops of rain began to fall, then he started on his little business trip and never had he failed to make it rain copiously. Friends of Don Jose Lopez, hearing all this talk, were not slow to take advantage of it. The time for the election of county officials was near and they promptly placed Don Jose in nomination for the office of the sheriff of San Miguel County.

When people applied to the parish priest for advice in this matter, he laughingly told them that he did not know if all these current rumors were true, quien sabe, but surely nothing was impossible before the Lord and the blessed saints, and Don Jose being a friend, he advised them to give him their support, as he was a very good and capable man who would make an ideal sheriff. To be sure, the Don paid his debts and was never remiss in his duties to Holy Church.

We crossed over the Raton Mountains and were then in the northern part of the Territory of New Mexico. What a curious country it was! The houses were built of adobe or sun-dried brick of earth, in a very primitive fashion. We seemed to be transported as by magic to the Holy Land as it was in the lifetime of our Saviour.

The architecture of the buildings, the habits and raiment of the people, the stony soil of the hills, covered by a thorny and sparse vegetation, the irrigated fertile land of the valleys, the small fields surrounded by adobe walls—all this could not fail to remind one vividly of descriptions and pictures of Old Egypt and Palestine. Here you saw the same dusty, primitive roads and quaint bullock carts, that were hewn out of soft wood and joined together with thongs of rawhide and built without the vestige of iron or other metal. There were the same antediluvian plows, made of two sticks, as used in ancient Egypt at the time of the Exodus, when Moses led the Jews out of captivity to their Promised Land. The very atmosphere, so dry and exhilarating, seemed strange. In this transparent air, objects which were twenty miles distant seemed to be no farther than two or three miles at most. In such a country it would not have surprised anyone to meet the Saviour face to face, riding an ass or burro over the stony road, followed by His disciples and a multitude of people, who, with the most implicit faith in the Lord's power to perform miracles, expected Him to provide them with an abundance of loaves and fishes. Here we were in a country, a territory of the United States, which was about eighteen hundred years behind the civilization of other Christian countries.

As we passed through the many little hamlets and towns, the male population, who were sitting on the shady side of their houses, regarded us with lazy curiosity. They were leaning against the cool, adobe walls, dreaming and smoking cigarettes. The ladies seemed to possess a livelier disposition and emerged from their houses to gossip and gather news. They viewed me with the greatest interest and curiosity and, shifting the mantillas, or rebozos, behind which they hid their faces after the Moorish fashion, they gazed at me with shining eyes. And I believe that I found favor with many, for they would exclaim, "M'ira que Americanito tan lindo, tan blanco!" (What a handsome young American. See what beautiful blue eyes he has and what a white complexion.) And mothers warned the maidens not to look at me, as I might have the evil eye. I heard one lady tell her daughter, "You may look at him just once, Dolores; oh, see how handsome he is!" (Valga me, Dios, que lindo es, pobrecito!)And the way the young lady gazed was a revelation to me. The fire of her limpid black eyes struck me as a ray of glorious light. An indescribable thrill, never before known, rose in my breast and she held me enthralled under a spell which I had not the least desire to break. And they said that it was I who had the evil eye! To say that these people were lacking in the virtues and accomplishments of modern civilization entirely would be a mistake very easily made indeed by strangers who, on passing through their land, did not understand their language and were unfamiliar with their social customs and mode of living. They extended unlimited hospitality to every one alike, to friend or stranger, to poor or rich. They were most charmingly polite in their conversation, personal demeanor, and social intercourse and very charitable and affectionate to their families and neighbors. These people are happy as compared with other nations in that they do not worry and fret over the unattainable and doubtful, but lightheartedly they enjoy the blessings of the present, such as they are. Therefore, if rightly understood, they may be the best of companions at times, being sincere and unselfish; so I have found many of them to be later on, during the intercourse of a more intimate acquaintance. In the large towns, as Santa Fe, Albuquerque, and Las Vegas, where there lived a considerable number of Americans, these would naturally associate together, as, for instance, the American colony in Paris or Berlin or other foreign places, so as not to be obliged to mingle with the natives socially any more than they chose. But in the village where my relatives lived, we had not the alternative of choosing our own countrymen for social companionship.

Therefore, I realized when I reached my destination that I had to change my accustomed mode of living and adapt myself to such a life as people had led eighteen hundred years ago. I thought that if I took the example of the Saviour's life for my guiding star, I would certainly get along very well. Undoubtedly this would have sufficed in a spiritual sense, but I found that it would be impractical as applied to my temporal welfare and the requirements of the present time. For I could not perform miracles nor could I live as the Saviour had done, roaming over the country and teaching the natives. And then, seeing that there were so many Jews in New Mexico, I feared they might attempt to crucify me and I did not relish the thought. Therefore I accepted King Solomon's life as the next best one to emulate. While I was greatly handicapped by not possessing the riches of the great old king, I fancied that I had a plenty of his wisdom, and although I could not cut as wide a swath as he had done, I did well enough under the circumstances. I was, of course, limited to a vastly smaller scale in the pursuit and enjoyment of the many good things to be had in New Mexico. Ever joyous, free from care, I drifted in my voyage of life with the stream of hope over the shining waters of a happy and delightful youth.

CHAPTER V.

ON THE RIO GRANDE. AN ABSTRACT OF THE
AUTHOR'S GENEALOGY OF MATERNAL LINEAGE

In the month of September I came to the end of my journey, as I arrived on the Rio Abajo. Now I began the second chapter of my life's voyage. No longer a precocious child, I was growing to young manhood and was not lacking in those qualities which are essential in the successful performance of life's continual struggle. I was heartily welcomed by my uncle, my mother's brother. My aunt, poor lady, had, of course, given me up as lost and greeted me with joyful admiration. But she did not venture close to me, for in me she saw a strong, lusty young man, bright eyed, alert-looking and carrying a deadly army revolver and wicked hunting knife at his belt. To be sure, I was suntanned and graybacked beyond comparison with the dust of a thousand miles of wagon road.

As I had expected, I found my uncle in very prosperous circumstances, in a commercial sense. And no wonder, for he was a tall, fine-looking man, under forty and overflowing with energy and personal magnetism. And my mother's little family tree did the rest—aye, surely, it was not to be sneezed at, as will be presently seen.

Of course, mother traced her ancestral lineage, as all other people do, to Adam and Eve in general, but in particular she claimed descent from those ancient heroes of the Northland, the Vikings. These daring rovers of the seas were really a right jolly set of men. In their small galleys they roamed the trackless seas, undaunted alike by the terrors of the hurricane as by the perils of unknown shores. On whatever coast they chanced—finding it inhabited, they landed, fought off the men and captured their women. They sacked villages and plundered towns, and loading their ships with booty, they set sail joyfully, homeward bound for the shores of the misty North

Sea, the shallow German Ocean. Here they had a number of retreats and strongholds. There was Helgoland, the mysterious island; Cuxhaven, at the mouth of the river Elbe; Buxtehude, notoriously known from a very peculiar ferocious breed of dogs; Norse Loch on the coast of Holstein, and numerous other locker, or inlets, hard to find, harder to enter when found and hardest to pronounce. In the course of time these rovers were visited by saintly Christian missionaries and, like all other Saxon tribes, they accepted the light of the Christian Gospel. They saw the error of their way and eschewed their vocation of piracy and devoted their energies to commerce and the spreading of the Gospel of Christ.

Piously they decorated the sails of their crafts and blazoned their war shields with the sign of the cross. They kidnapped holy priests (for otherwise they came not), and taking them aboard their ships, they sailed to their several ports. Then they forced the unwilling Fathers to unite them in holy wedlock to the maidens of their choice. To many havens they sailed, and in every one they had an only wife. They made their priests inscribe texts from the holy Gospel on pieces of parchment made from the skin of hogs, and instead of robbing people, as of yore, they paid with the word of Holy Scripture for the booty they levied. This, they said, was infinitely more precious than any worldly dross. All hail to the memory of my gallant maternal ancestor, who, when surfeited with the caresses of his Fifine of Normandy, flew to the arms of Mercedes of Andalusia. Next, perhaps, he appeared in Greenland, blubbering with an Esquimau heiress. Anon, you might have found him in Columbia in the tolls of a princely Pocahontas. In Mexico he ate the ardent chile from the tender hand of his Guadalupita, and later on he was on time at a five o'clock family tea party in Japan, or he might have kotowed pidgin-love to a trusting maid in a China town of fair Cathay. In Africa — oh, horror! — here I draw the veil, for in my mind's eye I behold a burly negro (yes, sah!) staring at me out of fishy, blue eyes. It is said of these gallant rovers of the seas that they were subject to a peculiar malady when on shore. It caused them to stagger and swagger, use violent language, and deport themselves not unlike people who are seized with mal de mer, or sickness of the sea. When attacked by this failing, their wives would cast them bodily into the holds of their ships and start them out to sea, where they soon recovered their usual health and equilibrium and continued on their rounds. They were the first of all commercial travelers and the hardiest, jolliest and most prosperous—but they did not hoard their earnings.

My uncle conducted a store, selling merchandise of every description. Dutch uncle though he was to me, I must give him thanks for the careful business training he bestowed on me. I say with pride that I proved to be his most apt and willing pupil. He taught me how the natives, by nature simple-minded and unsophisticated, had lost all confidence in their fellow-men in general and merchants in particular through the, to say the least, very dubious and suspicious dealings of the tribes of Israel. My uncle said he was an old timer in New Mexico, but the Jew was there already when he came and, added he, thoughtfully, "I believe the Jews came to America with Columbus." With a pack of merchandise strapped to his back, this king of commerce crossed the plains in the face of murderous Indians and with the unexplainable, crafty cunning of his race, he sold tobacco and trinkets to the warriors who had set out to kill him, and to the squaws he sold Parisian lingerie at a bargain. He swore that he was losing money and selling the goods below cost, not counting the freight.

As the Indians had no money and nothing else of commercial value to him, he bartered for the trophies of victory which the proud chiefs carried suspended from their belts. Deprecatingly he called their attention to the undeniable fact that these articles had been worn before and had to be rated as second-hand goods. But he hoped that his brother-in-law, Isaac Dreibein, who conducted a second-hand hairdressing establishment in New York City, would take these goods off his hands. This trade flourished for a time, until, as usual, Israel fell off from the Lord, by opening shop on the Sabbath. An unlucky Moses got into a fatal altercation with a Comanche chief, whom he cheated out of a scalplock, as he was as baldheaded as a hen's egg. Thereat the Indians became suspicious and refused to trade with the Jews ever after.

With proverbial German thoroughness, uncle instructed me in all the tricks and secrets of his profession. He had found that the Mexicans were good buyers, if handled scientifically, for they would never leave the store until they had spent all their money. Therefore, in order to encourage our customers, we kept a barrel of firewater under the counter as a trade starter. One or more drams of old Magnolia would start the ball to roll finely. Our merchandise cost mark was made up from the words, "God help us!" Every letter of this pious sentiment designated one of the numbers from one to nine and a cross stood for naught. When I said to uncle, "No wonder that our business prospers under this mark—God help us!—but say, who helps our customers?" he was nonplussed for a moment, and then he laughed heartily and said that this had never worried him yet.

There was not much money in circulation in New Mexico at that time, as the country was without railroads and too isolated to market farm produce, wool and hides profitably. Mining for gold was carried on at Pinos Altos, near the southern boundary, but the Apaches did not encourage prospecting to any extent. During the period of the discovery of gold in California, in the days of "forty-nine," the people of New Mexico had become quite wealthy through supplying the California placer miners with mutton sheep at the price of an ounce of gold dust per head, when muttons cost half a dollar on the Rio Grande. At that rate of profit they could afford the time and expense of driving their herds of sheep to market at Los Angeles, even though the Apaches of Arizona took their toll and fattened on stolen mutton.

CHAPTER VI.

INDIAN LORE. THE WILY NAVAJO

The principal source of the money supply was the United States Government, which maintained many forts and army posts in the Territories as a safeguard against the Apache and Navajo Indians. During the Civil War, the Navajo Indians broke out and raided the Mexican settlements along the Rio Grande and committed many outrages and thefts. The Government gave these Indians the surprise of their lives. An army detachment of United States California volunteers swooped suddenly down on the Navajos and surprised and conquered them in the strongholds of their own country. The whole tribe was forced to surrender, was disarmed, and transported to Fort Stanton by the Government.

This military reservation lies on the eastern boundary of New Mexico, on the edge of the staked plains of Texas. Here the Navajos were kept in mortal terror of their hereditary enemies, the Comanche Indians, for several years, and they were so thoroughly cowed and subdued by this stratagem that they were good and peacable ever after. The Government allowed them to reoccupy their native haunts and granted them a reservation of seventy-five miles square. These Indians are blood relatives to the savage Apaches. They speak the same language, as they are also of Mongolian origin. They came originally from Asia in an unexplained manner and over an unknown route. They have always been the enemies of the Pueblo Indians, who are descendants of the Toltec and Aztec races. Unlike the Pueblo Indians, who live in villages and maintain themselves with agricultural pursuits, the Navajos are nomads and born herdsmen.

The Navajo tribe is quite wealthy now, as they possess many thousands of sheep and goats, and they are famed for their quaint and beautiful blankets and homespun, which they weave on their hand looms from the wool of their sheep. They owned large herds of horses, beautiful ponies, a crossed breed of mustangs and Mormon stock, which latter they had stolen in their raids on the Mormon settlements in Utah. As saddle horses, these ponies are unexcelled for endurance under rough service.

Mentally the Navajo is very wide awake and capable of shrewd practices, as shown by the following incident, which happened to my personal knowledge.

A tall, gaudily appareled Indian, mounting a beautiful pony, came to town and offered for sale at our store several gold nuggets the size of hazelnuts. He took care to do this publicly, so as to attract the attention of some Mexicans, who became immensely excited at the sight of the gold and began to question him at once in order to ascertain how and whence he had obtained the golden nuggets. They almost fought for the privilege of taking him as an honored guest to their respective homes. The Indian was very non-committal as regarded his gold mine, but very willing to accept the sumptuous hospitality so freely rendered him. He was soon passed on from one disappointed Mexican to another, who in turn fared no better and invariably sped the parting guest to the door of his nearest neighbor. When the Indian had made the circuit of the town in this manner he looked very sleek and happy, indeed, but the people were no wiser. The knowledge of having been shamefully buncoed by an Indian and disappointed in their lust for gold made the Mexicans desperate. They held an indignation meeting and resolved to capture the wily Navajo and compel him, under torture, if necessary, to divulge the secret of his gold mine. Consequently, they overcame the Indian, and when they threatened him with torture and death, he yielded and said that he had found the gold in the Rio de San Francisco, a mountain stream of Arizona. He promised to guide them to the spot where he obtained the nuggets, saying that the bottom of the stream was literally covered with golden sand, which might be seen from a distance, as it shone resplendently in the sun. Then every able-bodied Mexican in town who possessed a horse prepared to join a prospecting expedition to the wild regions of mysterious Arizona. They organized a company and elected a captain, a man of courage and experience. The captain's first official act was to place a guard of four armed men over the Navajo to prevent his escape, otherwise they treated their prisoner well.

The women of the town cooked and baked for the party, and undoubtedly each lady reveled in the hope to see her own man return with a sackful of gold; and as a result of these fanciful expectations they were in the best of spirits, laughing and singing the livelong day.

At last the party was off, and what happened to them I shall relate, as told me by the captain, Don Jose Marie Baca y Artiaga, and in his own words as nearly as I can remember them. "Valga me, Dios, Senor! What an experience was that trip to Arizona! It began and ended with disappointment and disaster. All the men of our party seemed to have lost their wits from the greed of gold. They began by hurrying. Those who had the best mounts rushed on ahead, carrying the Indian along with them, and strove to leave their companions who were not so well mounted behind. The first night's camp had of necessity to be made at a point on the Rio Puerco, distant about thirty-five miles. As the last men rode into camp, the first comers were already making ready to leave again. In vain I remonstrated and commanded. There was a fight, and not until several men were seriously wounded came they to their senses and obeyed my orders. I threatened to leave them and return home, for I knew very well that unless our party kept together we were sure to be ambushed and attacked. I cautioned my companions as they valued their lives to watch the Navajo and shoot him on the spot at the first sign of treachery. This devil of an Indian led us over terrible trails, across the roughest and highest peaks and the deepest canyons of a wild, broken country. He seemed to be on the lookout ever for an opportunity to escape, but I did not give him the chance. Our horses suffered and were well-nigh exhausted when we finally sighted the coveted stream from a spur of the Mogollon range which we were then descending. The stream glistened and shone like gold in the distance, under the hot rays of a noonday sun and my companions would have made a dash for the coveted goal if their horses had not been utterly exhausted and footsore. As it was, I had the greatest trouble to calm them. Arriving at the last and steepest declivity of the trail, I succeeded in halting the party long enough to listen to my words. 'Companions,' I said, 'hear me before you rush on! I shall stay here with this Indian, whom you will first tie to this mesquite tree. Now you may go, and may the saints deliver you from your evil passion and folly. Mind you, senores, I claim an equal share with you in whatever gold you may find. If any one objects, let him come forth and say so now, man to man. I shall hold the trail for those among you who would haply choose to return. Forsooth, companions, I like not the actions of this Indian. Beware the Apache, senores; remember we are in the Tonto's own country!'

"From my position I witnessed the exciting race to the banks of the stream, and saw plainly how eagerly my companions worked with pick and pan. Hard they worked, but not long, for soon they assembled in the shade of a tree, and after a conference I saw them make the usual preparations for camping. Several men looked after the wants of the horses, others built fires, and four of the party returned toward me. 'What luck, Companeros!' I hailed them when they came within hearing distance. 'Senor Capitan, we have come for the Indian,' said the spokesman of the squad. 'And what use have you for the Indian?' I asked. 'We shall hang him to yonder tree,' they said, 'as a warning to liars and impostors.' Bueno, Caballeros, he deserves it. I deliver him into your hands under this condition, that you grant him a fair trial, as becomes men who being good Catholics and sure of the salvation of their souls may not, without just cause, consign a heathen to the everlasting fires of perdition.'

"Silently, stoically, the Indian suffered himself to be led to the place of his execution. After the enraged Mexicans had placed him under a tree with the noose of a riata around his neck, they informed him that he might now plead in the defense of his life if he had anything to say. 'Mexicans,' said the Navajo, 'I fear not death! If I must die, let it be by a bullet. I call the great Spirit, who knows the hearts of his people, to witness that I beg not for my life. I have not a split tongue nor am I an impostor. I have guided you to the place of gold. I have kept my promise. You Mexicans came with evil hearts. You fought your own brothers. You abandoned your sick companions on the trail to the coyote. You have broken the law of hospitality toward me, your guest, as no Spaniard has ever done before. Therefore, has your God punished you. He has changed the good gold of these waters to shimmering mica and shining dross. Fool gold He gives to fools! As you serve me now, so shall the

Apaches do to you. Never more shall you taste of the waters of the Rio Grande, so says the Spirit in my heart!'

"The Indian's dignified bearing and his inspired words on the threshold of eternity moved my conscience and caused a feeling of respect and pity for him in my breast as well as in others of our party. When Juan de Dios Carasco, who was known and despised by all for being a good-for-nothing thieving coward, drew his gun to shoot the Navajo in the back, I could not control my anger. 'Stop,' I shouted, 'you miserable hen thief, or you die at my hands, and now. This Indian should die, but not in such a manner. Senores, you have made me your capitan. Now I shall enforce my orders at the risk of my life's blood. Give that Indian a knife and fair play in a combat against the prowess of the valiant Don Juan de Dios Carasco.'

"Although greatly disconcerted, Juan de Dios had to toe the mark. There was no alternative for him now, as I was desperate and my orders were obeyed to the letter, for death was the penalty for disobedience. The fight between the Mexican and the Indian ended by the Navajo, who was sorely wounded, throwing his knife into the heart of his enemy. It was a fair fight, although we accorded Juan de Dios, he being a Christian, this advantage against the Indian (who was better skilled in the use of weapons) that we allowed him to wrap his coat about his left arm as a shield, while the Indian was stripped to his patarague, or breechclout. We buried the body and allowed the Indian to shift for himself. I observed him crawling near the water's edge in quest of herbs, which he masticated and applied to his wounds with an outer coating of mud from the banks of the stream. During the following night he disappeared. I suspect that the golden nuggets which caused all our troubles were taken from the body of a prospector who had been murdered in the lonesome mountains of Arizona.

"We allowed our horses several days' rest to recuperate before starting on our return trip. You saw, senor, how we arrived. Starved, sore, and discouraged, we straggled home, jeered at and ridiculed by wiseacres who are always ready to say, 'I told you so!' and by enemies who had no liking for us. But the women, may Santa Barbara keep them virtuous! they who loved their husbands truly rejoiced to welcome us home, although we failed to bring them chispas de oro.

"As concerns the wife of Juan de Dios, and who was now his widow, pobrecita, she was not to be found at her home. She had taken advantage of her man's absence to decamp to the mountain of Manzana with a strapping goat-herder, a very worthy young man, whom she loved and is now happily free to marry."

CHAPTER VII.

THE FIGHT IN THE SAND HILLS. THE PHANTOM DOG

A number of years had I lived with my relatives when uncle found it expedient to sell out his business. He had prospered wonderfully in his commercial ventures. Long since had his coffers absorbed most of the money circulating within his sphere of trade. Thereafter he accepted commercial paper in payment for merchandise, and trade grew immensely. Our customers soon learned how easy it was to affix their signatures to promissory notes and to mortgages on their lands or cattle, their horses, sheep, crops, and chattels. Of course there was a little interest to be paid on the indebtedness, but as it was merely a trifling one and a half per centum per month or eighteen per cent yearly, it was of no consequence. And it was so easy to pay your debts. Just think of it, people bought everything they needed and longed for at the store and paid for it by simply signing their names to several papers. When the day of payment came, they could liquidate their debts by renewing their obligations. They simply signed a new set of similar papers with the interest compounded and added to the original debt. Surely Don Guillermo was conceded to stand highest in popular estimation of any set of men who had ever come to the Rio Grande. Had he not shown the people how to do business in a convenient and easy manner? Under such a system nobody worried or labored very much and life was like a pleasant dream. But alas! there has always been a beginning and an ending to everything under the sun, good or evil. The awakening from an easy life's dream was occasioned by a crushing blow. It fell on the day of final reckoning, when Don Guillermo, my good uncle, thought the time was propitious to realize something tangible on sundry duly signed, sealed, and witnessed instruments. There was a rumpus; neither earthquake nor cyclone would have caused a greater commotion in the community. What, then, did this lying gringo mean by resorting to the trickery of the United States law courts and the power and services of the county sheriff? Why did he wrest their property from them? Had this gringo not always accepted their signatures as a legal tender for the payment of their debts? Had he not told them time and again that their handwriting was better than gold? If uncle had fallen into the clutches of these furious people, he would undoubtedly have been lynched. But he had wisely disposed of all his property in the country and had left with his family for the States. I remained in the service of the buyer of and successor to his business.

Soon after I began to feel lonesome, restless and dissatisfied, and that life among the natives was not as pleasant and satisfactory as formerly may be easily imagined. In fact, the gringos were now cordially hated and envied by a certain class, the element of greatest influence among the people. This produced a feeling of unpleasantness not to be overcome, and I resolved to emigrate to California, overland, by way of Arizona. I longed for the companionship of people of my own race and wanted to see more of the world. There was an opportunity to go to a mining town of northern Arizona, with several ox-teams which were freighting provisions. The freighter, Don Juan Mestal, assured me that he was very glad to have the pleasure and comfort of my company and would not listen to an offer of remuneration on my part. He said there was the choice of two routes; one road passed through the country of the Navajo Indians and the other road led past Zuhl, the isolated Pueblo village. Don Juan said that he would not go by way of Zuni, if he could avoid it, as he was prejudiced against this tribe. Not that they were hostile or dangerous, but he had acquired a positive aversion, amounting to abhorrence, for those peaceful people when he, as a boy, accompanied his father on a trading expedition there. At that time he witnessed the revolting execution of a score of Navajos who had been apprehended as spies by the Zunis. These unfortunates came to their village as visiting guests, it being in the time of the harvest of maize, when these Indians celebrate their great Thanksgiving feast. A young Navajo chief, who led the visiting party, aroused the ire of the old medicine chief of the tribe, who had lately added a new attraction to his household, beshrewing himself with another lovely young squaw. It was said that the enamored damsel had made preparations to elope with the gallant Navajo chief, but was betrayed by the telltale barking of the dogs, great numbers of which infest all Indian villages. The old doctor accused the Navajos of espionage and had them taken by surprise and imprisoned in an underground foul den. Then met the chiefs of the tribe in their estufa, or secret meeting place, to pass judgment on the culprits. The old medicine chief smoked himself into a trance in order to receive special instructions from the great Spirit regarding the degree of punishment to be inflicted on the unlucky Navajos. After sleeping several hours, he awoke and announced that he had dreamed the Navajos were to be clubbed to death. After sunrise the next morning these poor Indians met their doom in the public square of the village unflinchingly in the presence of the whole population.

They were placed in a row, facing the sun, about ten feet apart. A Zuni executioner, armed with a war club, was stationed in front of each victim, and another one, armed likewise, stood behind him. A war chief raised his arms and yelled, and forty clubs were raised in air. Then the great war drum, or tombe, boomed out the knell of death. There was a sickening, crashing thud, and twenty Navajos fell to earth with crushed skulls, each cabeza having been whacked simultaneously, right and left, fore and aft, by two stone clubs in the hands of a pair of devils.

It had always been an enigma to me that the Pueblo Indians, who were not to be matched as fighters against the Apache and Navajo had been able to defend their villages against the onslaught of these fierce tribes, their hereditary enemies. Don Juan Mestal enlightened me on that topic. He said the explanation therefor was to be found in a certain religious superstition of the Navajos and Apaches, which circumstance the Pueblo Indians took advantage of and exploited to the saving of their lives. When they had reason to expect an attack on their villages, the Pueblo laid numerous mines and torpedoes on all the approaches and streets of their towns. While these mines did not possess the destructive power of dynamite or gunpowder, they were equally effective and powerful, and never failed to repulse the enemy, especially if reinforced by hand grenades of like ammunition, thrown by squaws and pappooses from the flat roofs of their houses. By some means or other it had become known to the descendants of Montezuma that when an Apache stepped on something out of the ordinary "he scented mischief" and believed himself unclean and befouled with dishonor, and fancied himself disgraced before God and man; and forthwith he would hie himself away to do penance at the shrine of the nearest water sprite. This superstition they brought from Asia, their native land.

When the day of our departure drew near, I visited my numerous friends to bid them farewell and receive many like wishes in return. I must own that I felt a pang of sadness when I saw tears well up in the innocent eyes of sweet maidens and saw the fires dimmed in the black orbs of lovely matrons whom I had held often in my arms to the measure and tuneful melody of the fantastic wild fandango; musical Andalusian strains which words cannot describe—soul-stirring, enchanting, promising and denying, plaintive or jubilant, songs from Heaven or wails from the depths of Hades. Here I lived the happiest hours of my life, but being young, I did not realize it then.

When I came to the house of Don Reyes Alvarado, who was my chum and bosom friend, and also of like age, he gave me a pleasant surprise. He informed me that there would be a dance at the Han-cho Indian's settlement that same night, one of those ceremonial events which I had long desired to attend in order to study the customs and habits of these descendants of the Aztecs. Their social dances are inspired by ancient customs and are the outbursts of the dormant, barbaric rites of a religion which these people were forced to abandon by their conquering masters, the Spaniards. Outwardly and visibly Christians, taught to observe the customs of the Roman Catholic Church and to conform to its ritual, these people, who were the scum and overflow from villages of Pueblo Indians, were yet Aztec heathens in the consciousness of their souls and inclination of their hearts.

Shortly after sunset we were on our way to the sand dunes of the Rio Grande, where these poor outcasts had squatted and built their humble homes of terron, or sod, which they cut from the alkali-laden soil of the vega. They held their dance orgies in the estufa, the meeting house of the tribe. This was a long, low structure built of adobe, probably a hundred feet long and nine feet wide, inside measure. The building was so low that I could easily lay the palm of my uplifted hand against the ceiling of the roof, which was made of beams of cottonwood, covered with sticks off which the bark had been carefully peeled, the whole had then been covered with clay a foot in depth. The floor of this long, low tunnel-like room was made of mud which had been skilfully tampered with an admixture of short cut straw and had been beaten into the proper degree of hardness. Dampened at intervals, this floor was quite serviceable to dance on. There were no windows or ventilators in this hall and only one door at the end. This was made out of a slab of hewn wood and was just high and wide enough to admit a good sized dog. The hall was brilliantly lighted by a dozen mutton tallow dips, which were distributed about the room in candelabra of tin, hanging on the mud-plastered and whitewashed walls. The orchestra consisted of one piece only, an ancient war drum, or tombe, and was located at the farther end of the room. It was beaten by an Indian, who was, if possible, more ancient than the drum. As we approached we heard the muffled sound of the drum within. "Caramba, amigo!" said my friend; "they are at it already, and judging from the sound, they are very gay to-night. Madre santissima! I remember that this is a great night for these Indians, as it is the anniversary of the Noche Triste, which they celebrate in commemoration of the Aztec's victory over the Spaniards when the Indians almost wiped their enemies off the face of the earth. Senor, to tell the truth, rather would I turn my horse's head homeward. Pray, let us return!" "And why, amigo," I asked. "Because this has always been a day of ill luck for our family," said Don Reyes. "It began with the misfortune of the famed Knight Don Pedro Alvarado, the bravest of men and the right hand of Don Fernando Cortez. In the bloody retreat of the Spaniards from Mexico, in their fight with the Aztecs, during the Noche Triste, Don Pedro Alvarado, from whom we were descended, lost his mare through a deadly arrow. "Muy bien, amigo Don Reyes," said I; "if you fear these people, I advise you to return home to Dona Josefita, but I shall go on alone." "I fear not man or beast!" flared up Don Reyes, "as you well know, friend, but these are heathen fiends, not human, who worship a huge rattlesnake, which they keep in an underground den and feed with the innocent blood of Christian babes. Lead on, senor, I shall follow. I see it is as Dona Josefita, my little wife, says: "If these young gringos crave a thing, there is no use in denying them, for they seem to compel! To the very door of that uncanny place I follow you, amigo, but enter therein I shall not, unless I be first absolved from my sins and shriven by the padre."

We had now arrived at the door of the estufa (oven), where the entertainment was going on, full blast. I alighted and my friend took charge of my horse and stationed himself at the door while I got down on all fours and crawled inside. I seated myself on a little bench at one side of the entrance. When my eyes got accustomed to the dense atmosphere of the place, I observed that the room was full of people, dancing in couples with a peculiar slow-waltz step. The ladies stayed in their places while the men made the rounds of the hall. After a few turns with a lady, they shuffled along to the next one, continually exchanging their partners. As the dancers passed me by, one after another, they noticed me, and many among them scowled and looked angry and displeased. Suddenly the drum stopped for a few minutes. Then it began in a faster tempo. Now the men remained stationary, while the ladies made the circuit of the room and each one in her turn passed in front of me. They looked lovely in their costumes of finely embroidered snow-white single garments, trimmed with many silver ornaments and trinkets and in their short calico skirts and beautiful moccasins. Their limbs were tastefully swathed in white buckskin leggins, which completed the costume.

Faster and faster beat the drum, and the sobbing, rhythmic sound thrilled my senses and filled my heart with an indescribable weird, fierce longing. I saw a maiden approach taller and finer than the rest. One glance of her soft, wild eyes and I flew to her arms. "Back, Indians!" I shouted, "honor your queen!" and entered the lists of the frolicsome dance. Wilder beat the drum and faster. As the old Indian warmed to his work, he broke out in a doleful, monotonous song, the words of which I did not understand. It sounded to me like this:

Anna-Hannah—
Anna-Hannah—
May-Ah!—
Anna-Hannah-Sarah-Wah!
Moolow-Hoolow, Ji-Hi-Tlack!
Anna-Hannah—
May-Ah-Ha!

So it went on indefinitely.

To lay this troubled spirit I tossed him a handful of coins, with the unfortunate result that his guttural song became, if anything, more loud and boisterous. I had no thought of exchanging my partner, as the Aztec maiden clung to me. With closed eyes and parted lips she moved as in a blissful dream. I have known Christian people become frantic under the impetus of great religious excitement and I have seen them act very strangely, also have I seen Indians similarly affected during their medicine-ghost dances. Now I, who had not thought it possible of myself, had become more savage and uncontrollable than any one. I suppose it was the irritating, monotonous sound of the war drum that did it, jarring my nerves, and the peculiar Indian odor in the stifling hot air of the close room, enhanced by the exhilarating sensation of threatening danger, and that in the presence of the adored sex. Assuredly all this was more than enough to set me off, as I am naturally impulsive and of a high-strung nervous temperament.

I must say that considering the modest costumes of these Indian ladies and their bashful and shrinking disposition, it does seem strange that they should fascinate one like myself of the Saxon race. To be sure the sight of the bared shoulders and necks of society belles when undressed in the decollete fashion of their ball gowns ravishes and gluts our sensuality, but a momentary glimpse of the Indian maid's brown knee flashing by during the excitement of the fandango is just as suggestive, and the inch of hand-made embroidery on the edge of their short skirts is as effective as priceless lace on gowns of worth. And the Indian fashion has this to recommend it, that it is the less expensive of the two costumes. Ever watchful, ever on the alert, I saw the sheen of a knife flash from its scabbard in the hazy air, and my beautiful partner shivered and moaned in my arms. "Dog of an Indian, dare and die," shouted I, angrily. Four times I made the circuit of the room, and when again opposite the entrance of this man-kennel, I heard the voice of my faithful friend, Don Reyes Alvarado, calling me anxiously. I gave my lovely partner in charge of her tender-hearted sisters, for the poor wild thing had fainted and lay limply in my arms. The strong arm of my companion grasped me and drew me out into the fresh air, where I almost collapsed, overcome.

"Surely, amigo," said Reyes, "you will not blame me now for not entering, but you have endurance, for Dios! I should not have survived so long. Thank God you came out alive! When I saw them pass in knives, I had my doubts and momentarily expected to hear the report of your revolver. But when I saw you pass by infatuated with Jtz-Li-Cama, the cacique's daughter and wife of the murderous scoundrel, El Macho, then I gave you up. Oh, see what is happening now. Amigo, you have broken up the dance. So it seemed. The drum was silent now and we heard the voices of men arguing in the Aztec idiom. Of a sudden the lights were extinguished and the crowd came out with a rush, and silently they stole away in the darkness.

"Now, amigo," said Reyes, "let me tell you something, which may haply serve you well. Knowing that an American accomplishes things which a Mexican like myself must let alone, I advise you to try for the hidden treasure of La Gran Quivira. Seeing that you are in the good graces of Jtz-Li-Cama, you might prevail with the cacique to guide you. He is said to be the only living man who knows the secret of the trove in the ruins of the sacred temple of the ancient city. The Indians believe that this treasure, which the Aztecs hid from the Spaniards, is guarded by a terrible phantom dog, the specter of one of the great dogs of Fernando Cortez which ravened among their Aztec ancestors. They fear the specter of this fabled Perro de la Malinche more than anything else on earth, as it is said to harrow their souls in Hades as it ravened their bodies when in the flesh."

After smoking a few cigarritos, my friend proposed to ride home, as there was really nothing else to be done. We rode slowly along, enjoying the beautiful night of this faultless climate, and I shall ever remember this night to my last day. There was a pleasant, refreshing odor in the air, the scent of the wild thyme which grows in these sand dunes. The moon rose over the Manzana range and flooded the broad valley with its soft, silvery rays. Suddenly, at a sharp turn of the trail, we found ourselves surrounded by silent forms arisen from the misty ground. "Don Reyes Alvarado," spoke the voice of the Indian, known as the macho, "I have come for revenge and am now ready to wipe out the insults you heaped on me when you charged me with the theft of your calves. I challenge thee to fight.

Alight from thy horse, cowardly Spaniard! To-night of all nights shalt thou feel the Indians' blade between thy ribs." "Fight him, amigo," I said. "I shall enforce fair play." But my friend Reyes whom I knew to be a man of both strength and courage, weakened, being cowed with the superstition of the unlucky Noche Triste. "Tomorrow I shall fight thee, Indian," he answered "not at nighttime, like a thieving coyote." "If thou wert not astride thy horse and out of my reach, thou wouldst not dare say that to me, thou cuckold dupe of the Americans!" sneered the Indian. This insult to my companion angered me, and I demanded a retraction and an apology therefor from the Indian. When the macho flatly refused and repeated the insult in a more aggravating manner, I replied that I feared not to meet him or any other goatherding Indian and was ready to fight him on the spot.

Saying this, I dismounted and threw my horse's bridle to my friend Reyes to hold. Then the cacique, or Pueblo chief, the father of Jtz-Li-Cama, appeared and demanded our weapons. "I shall not interfere in this fight, senores," said he, "if you surrender your weapons to me, the lawful alguacil (officer) of this district." He then took the macho's knife, and I gave him my revolver and stripped for the fray.

I advanced and scratched a circle of about twelve feet diameter in the deep sand with my foot, then I stepped to the center of this ring and awaited my antagonist. I cautioned my friend Reyes to see to it that no one else overstepped the line. To the lonely sand dunes of the Rio Grande unwittingly I thus introduced the manly sport of the prize ring. But the battle was not fought for lucre or fame, nor according to the London Prize Ring Rules; it was fought in defense of a friend's honor, and the stake was life or death. The Indian made a rush for me, but I avoided him and warded off his blows. I did not touch him till I saw my chance, and then I tapped him under the chin which sent him sprawling. He arose promptly and came for me in a rage, when I felled him with a blow on the head. Again he came, and this time he gave me a stunning blow in the face, which maddened me so, that I took the offensive and laid him low with a terrific hit. I was now thoroughly infuriated and threw all caution to the winds. When he arose once more, I attacked him. He took to his heels and I followed him up. I noticed then that the whole crowd of

Indians were running after us, but I had now become reckless and did not mind. Then I stumbled over a root and fell face down in the sand. Before I could arise fully the macho had turned and thrown himself upon me. I managed to turn over on my back and gripped him by throat and face, so that he was really in my power, and I felt that he was subdued so that I could easily force him under, and, small wonder, for with the terrible grip of my hand had I once crushed a man's fingers in a wrestling match. Now I used the macho's body as a shield against the furious onslaught of his people, who attacked me with rocks, clubs, and anything they could lay hands to. I thought, and I never ceased thinking and planning for one moment, that the affair looked very serious for me, when I saw the cacique approach with my pistol in hand, exclaiming, "Now, gringo, thou shalt die, on the altar of the god, at the sacred shrine of Aztlan, I shall lay thy quivering heart!" In vain I looked for help from my companion, who had sought safety in flight. Something had to be done and that quickly. Surely I had one trusty friend, true as steel, who would not forsake me in the extremity of my peril. I bethought me of my little "American bulldog" which I had picked up in the cars in Kansas, and which had ever since followed me faithfully. "Sic-semper-Cerberus-Sic!" My right hand stole to my hip, a short sharp bark, and the treacherous cacique fell over with a crimson stain on his forehead. At the same moment a weird, uncanny yelp pierced the night, and a tremendous shaggy phantom cloud obscured the slender sickle of the moon. Terrified, the Indians screamed "El Perro! El Perro de la Malinche!" and shrilly the voices of frightened squaws took up the refrain, "Perro! Perro! Gringo Perro!"

When I staggered to my feet, I was alone, sorely bruised and wounded, but master of the field. I recovered my revolver, which lay at my feet and contrived to mount my horse, whose bridle had caught on the greasewood brush, and I headed for home.

Not long thereafter I met my friend Reyes, who was followed by a retinue of peons. "Gracias a Dios. Amigo!" he exclaimed, on seeing me. "I came after your body, if it were to be found, and here you are alive. When I heard the report of firearms and knowing that those devils had your weapon, I feared the worst. How on earth did you manage to escape them? Seeing you down and beset by the whole tribe, I gave you up for dead and fled."

I told my friend that with God's help and the phantom dog's assistance I had beaten off my assailants, and I thought that the cacique had been sorely bitten by the dog. Dona Josefita was very anxious and excited. When she saw me coming, she cried, "The saints preserve us, oh here he is! Mercy, how he looks, pobrecito! he is cut all to pieces. Hurry, Reyes, bring him in here and lay him gently down. Hombre, husband, coward! how couldst thou abandon thy friend who fought for thy honor, not fearing the death. I wager that pale hussy, Jtz-Li-Cama, was, as usual, the cause of this strife between men!"

The kind lady then attended deftly and skillfully to the dressing of my wounds, applying soothing herbs and healing ointments, which tended to allay the fever, and she nursed me with the tenderest care, so that in a week's time I was as well as ever, though not without a feeling of regret for my too speedy recovery.

Of course, there arose the rumor of a fierce battle between Americans and Indians. To silence this silly talk and to avoid unpleasant complications, I surrendered myself to the alcalde of the precinct and accused myself of having disturbed the peace of the realm. Pleading my case, I stated that as there was nobody but the peace disturbers involved, and as said parties did not make any further claim upon the Honorable Court, therefore, under the statute of the Territory and the Constitution of the United States, the law required that the court mulct the guilty parties in the payment of a nominal fine and discharge the culprits. The Honorable Court decreed that I as an American ought to know the American law best, and discharged me after I paid my self-imposed fine. The administering of justice in cases of importance was, of course, relegated to the United States Circuit Courts, but Uncle Sam did not care to meddle with the many troublesome alcaldes or justices of the peace, as he did not understand the Spanish language very well. This was certainly humiliating and embarrassing, but who can blame him, as no one is over anxious to be rated an ignorant person.

My Mexican friends decided to give a farewell party in my honor. Accordingly they made great preparations. They secured the largest sala, or hall, in the township and scoured the country for musicians—fiddlers and guitar players. Every person of any social notability was invited. They drew the line of social respectability at peons, or bondmen. This was a happy-go-lucky caste of people who possessed no property nor anything else, and consequently they had no cares and were under no responsibility of any kind, as the wealthier classes, who virtually owned them, had to provide for their necessities. The system of peonage in New Mexico had been abolished with the abolition of slavery in the United States, but the peons did not realize the wretchedness of their deplorable social status, and in their ignorance they regarded their bondage as a privilege, believing themselves fortunate to have their wants provided for by their patrones. They were treated kindly by their masters and looked upon as poor relations and intimate but humble friends.

The entertainment was to be of the velorio (wake) type, which begins as a prayer meeting and ends in a dance. My friends exerted themselves to the utmost to make this event the social climax of the season. They sent a committee to the pueblo of Isleta for several goatskins full of native wine, and incidentally they borrowed San Augustin, the pueblo's famous image saint, who they intended should preside over the velorio. As this prayer meeting was to be in my honor and for the sake of invoking the protection of the saints on my journey, they thought it best to procure San Augustin, who being the patron saint of the heathen Isleta Indians, would not mind giving a heretic Protestant gringo a good send-off, as he was accustomed to deal with heresy. They also procured a dozen fat mutton sheep, which were to be barbecued and served with chile pelado to the invited guests, surely a tempting menu and hot! The ladies baked bollos, tamales and frijoles. Melons and cantaloupes were brought in by the cartload. I was waited upon by a committee and received a formal invitation; for everything was done in grand Spanish style. When I arrived at the festive hall the ceremonies began. The ladies knelt before San Augustin, praying and chanting alternately. I took my customary station at the door, as master of the artillery. At the singing of a certain stanza and after the words, "Angeles, y Seraphim es! Santo! Santo! Santo!" I received my cue from one of the deacons who gave the order: "Fuego, maestro!" and I discharged my double barreled shotgun and a brace of six shooters in lightning-like succession. Surely this was pious devotion, properly emphasized, and it kept San Augustin from falling asleep. I used up a pound of gunpowder that night, and this was said to have been the grandest, most successful velorio ever held in that part of the world. At eleven o'clock I announced that my battery was overheated and too dangerous to reload, which stopped the praying and the grand baile began. There were several hundred dancing couples, who enjoyed themselves to the utmost until sunrise, and nobody thought of leaving for home until everything eatable and liquid was disposed of.

Now the date of our departure had arrived, and very sad, indeed, was I to leave these people who had done their very best to make me feel at home with them and who seemed to be really fond of me. I consoled Dona Josefita somewhat with the promise that I would return some day and find her the treasure of La Gran Quivira. Don Juan Mestal, the freighter, seemed as reluctant to leave as I was; something was always turning up to delay our start. But at last we were off.

After three days of travel, we came to a small town, where I met a Mexican whom I knew on the Rio Grande, where he had formerly lived. He invited me cordially to the wedding of his sister, which was to be on the next day at old Fort Wingate, an abandoned fort, and then a Mexican settlement. This man said that he had come on purpose to meet me, as he had heard of my intentions to leave the country. Although I did not like the man, who was said to be jealous of Americans, I accepted his urgent invitation more from curiosity to learn what he meant to do than for other reasons.

The next morning I started early from camp and rode over to the little town, distant fifteen miles. When I arrived in front of my prospective host's house I caught a glimpse of two men, who were sneaking off toward an old corral. Then I knew what was in the wind, for those two men were known to me as desperate cutthroat thieves and highwaymen; their specialty was to waylay and murder American travelers. My kind friend professed to be overmuch delighted at my arrival. He took charge of my horse and invited me into his house, where I met the bridal couple and their friends, who were carousing and gambling. I joined and made merry with them.

At ten o'clock the whole party made ready to proceed to the chapel, where the marriage ceremony was to be performed. I simulated the part of a very inebriated person, a condition which they looked forward to with hope and satisfaction, and told them that I would stay at the house to await their return. When everybody had left I thought I might as well get under way, feeling lonesome. I went out and around to the rear of the house, where the corral was, to get my horse, but found the gate fastened with chains and securely locked. The corral walls were built of adobe, and the two walls of it were a continuation of the side walls of the house, and its end wall formed an enclosure or backyard. My horse was there, and I found my saddle in one of the rooms of the building, hidden under a blanket. I entered the corral through the back door of the house, caught and saddled my horse, and then led him out to the street. This was a very laughable manner of leave-taking. The house was cut up into a labyrinth of small rooms, just large enough for a horse to turn around in, and the doors were low and narrow. As I could not find the outer door, I led my horse successively into every room in the house.

There is no furniture such as we use in a typical Spanish dwelling, no bedsteads, tables, or chairs. The inmates squat on divans arranged on the floor around the walls of the rooms, and at nighttime they spread their bedding on the floors. Some of the rooms were nicely carpeted with Mexican rugs. My horse must have thought he had come to a suite of stables, for he acted accordingly. He nosed around after grain and hay, whinnied and pawed, and seemed to enjoy himself generally. At last I found the right door, came out into the street and rode to the church to tender my best wishes to the happy couple and bid them adios. When the party emerged from the chapel they seemed to be very much surprised at seeing me. I told my host that I regretted to leave them so early in the day, but had an appointment to keep elsewhere. I would ride slowly out of town so that they could overtake me easily, should they wish to see me later, but nobody came, and after several hours I caught up with my companions.

CHAPTER VIII.

WITH THE NAVAJO TRIBE

After a couple of days we came to Fort Wingate, which controls the Navajo Indian Reservation. We camped here for a day to have some repair work done to our wagons, and I took a stroll over the hills after rabbits and returned to camp at nightfall. Don Juan told me that he had been visited by a number of Indians, who had bartered him some blankets and buckskins and he was highly pleased thereat.

The next morning we started early and traveled until noon. Several Indians had been following us for some time, and as soon as we made camp they squatted at our fire, while others were continually arriving, some afoot, but most of them on horseback. Manuelito, a grand-looking chief, rode into camp on the finest Indian pony I had ever seen. It was beautifully caparisoned; the saddle, bridle, and trappings were covered with silver mountings. This was by far the most gorgeously dressed Navajo I had ever met. He wore tight-fitting knickerbockers of jet-black buckskin, which resembled velvet, with a double row of silver buttons, set as close as possible on the outward seams, from top to bottom. On his legs from knee to ankle he wore homespun woolen stockings and his feet were covered by beaded moccasins of yellow, smoke-tanned buckskin. His bright red calico shirt was literally covered with silver ornaments and his ears were pierced with heavy silver rings, at least three inches in diameter. His wrists and arms were heavy with massive silver bracelets and others, carved from a stone, which resembled jade. About his neck he wore strings of wampum and glass beads, garnets, and bits of turquoise. The turquoise and garnet is found here in places known only to these Indians. His fingers were encircled by many rings, but the finest ornament he possessed was his body belt of great disks of silver, the size of tea saucers. All this jewelry was of a fair workmanship, such as is made by Navajo silversmiths out of coin silver. In fact, these Indians prefer silver to gold for purposes of personal adornment. The blanket which this

Indian wore around his waist was worth at least two hundred dollars; never have I seen its equal in beauty of pattern and texture.

The chief dismounted and withdrew with Don Juan behind a wagon for a talk, as I presumed. They reappeared soon, and the chief mounted his steed and cavorted around our camp as one possessed. Furiously lashing his horse, he scattered our cooking utensils and acted in a most provoking manner generally. I noticed then that the noble chief was intoxicated, and when I questioned Don Juan sharply, he admitted that he had given the Indian some whiskey, and on the day before as well. I warned the Don to have no further dealings with these Indians and advised him to break camp at once in order to avoid trouble. I informed him also that he had committed a serious crime by selling liquor to Indians and that he was liable to be arrested at any time should a patrol from the fort happen our way. As the Mexican was frightened now, we took to the road in a hurry and traveled until a late hour that night. In fact, we did not stop until the cattle were exhausted.

Hardly had we prepared our camp and were sitting around our fire, when a horde of Indians appeared, clamoring for whiskey. As they were armed and threatening, Don Juan became so terrified that he climbed to the interior of a wagon to comply with the demand of the savages. When I saw this, I drew my rifle from its place under my bedding and placed it in readiness. Plainly I saw Don Juan come out of the wagon with the mischievous stone jug, as this happened in the bright light of our camp fire. That will never do, thought I, and quickly drawing my revolver, I persuaded the Don to drop the jug, incidentally smashing it with a 44 caliber bullet, taking care not to hurt anybody; and this was easily done, as the jug was a large one, it held three gallons. Instantaneously I grabbed my Winchester, and with my back against a wagon stood ready for action. The Indians uttered a howl of disappointment when they saw the jug collapse and its precious contents wasted, but were silenced by an exclamation of their chief. After an excited pow-wow between themselves, they disappeared among the hills in the shadows of the night.

"Muchas gracias, senor Americana," said Don Juan, "quien sabe?" What would have happened if the Indians had gotten the liquor, which I dared not refuse them; but I think this ends our troubles. We passed a sleepless night, and long before sunrise Don Juan made preparations for our departure.

When the herders rounded up the cattle, they found that several yoke of oxen were missing, and greatly alarmed, they said that they believed the Indians had stolen them during the night. Don Juan did not appear to be very anxious to search for the missing cattle himself, so he sent out the herders again after breakfast. They returned with the report of having found the tracks of Indians who had apparently driven the cattle toward the hills, and stated that they were afraid to follow, fearing for their lives.

As it was nearly noon by this time, we cooked our dinner, and while doing so were visited again by a number of the Indians. Don Juan intimated to them that several of his oxen had strayed off during the night, and the Navajos kindly offered to go in search of them for a remuneration. They demanded a stack of tortillas a foot high and a sack of flour. Nolens-volens, squatted Don Mestal before the fire and baked bread for the wily Indians as a ransom for his cattle. Of course then the missing oxen were soon brought up, and we lost no time in getting under way.

Until midnight we traveled, as Don Juan was very anxious to get away from the reservation of these Indians, which is seventy-five miles across. This night we experienced a repetition of the tactics of the night before, as regarded the safety of our herd, but Don Juan had to pay a higher ransom in the morning. While we were awaiting the arrival of the Indians with our lost steers, Chief Manuelito honored us again with his presence. He sat down at our fire, and producing a greasy deck of Spanish playing cards, he challenged Don Juan to a game of monte. That was an irresistible temptation for my companion. By the smiling expression of his wizened features I divined that he thought he saw his chance for revenge. Manuelito undoubtedly had a strain of sporting blood in his veins, as he offered to stake his horses, blankets, squaws, and everything he had against the Mexican's wagons and cargo. I warned Don Juan to have a care, as I knew the cunning of the Navajo tribe, having dealt with them before, and advised him to play the traps he had bought from them with liquor against a chipper little squaw who was richly dressed and had come with Chief Manuelito, mounted on a white pony. I believed her to be the chief's daughter. When she understood the import of the conversation, she looked haughtily and in a disdainful manner at Don Juan, but appeared to be pleased with me and eyed me with symptoms of curiosity. Of course, I expected her to defy Don Juan to take her, and simply ride off in case he should win the game. At any rate, I meant to take her under my protection, if necessary, and send her home to her people. In fact, the liquor which Don Juan had sold these Indians had belonged to me and had been presented to me by a friend as an antidote for possible snake bites on the road to Arizona.

The gambling began, and my Mexican companions became so engrossed in the enjoyment of their alluring national game of monte that they forgot everything else. The drivers were as interested as their employer and bet the poor trinkets they possessed on the result of the game. There arrived more Indians continually, and I observed a familiar face amongst these and saw that I myself was recognized. The game was ended as I had foreseen, with Don Juan as the loser. He was an easy prey for these Indians, who are as full of tricks as the ocean is of water.

Then Chief Manuelito, who was highly elated with his victory over the Mexican, challenged me to a game in a very overbearing and provoking manner. I replied that I despised the game of monte, which was perhaps good enough for Mexicans and Indians, but was decided by chance; I boasted that I was ready to bet anything I had on my skill at shooting with the rifle, and challenged him and his whole tribe to the sport which was worthy of men, a shooting match. I think Manuelito would have accepted my challenge without hesitation and in great glee if he had not been restrained by the Indian whom I have mentioned before as having just arrived and recognized me. This Indian said something to the chief, which seemed to interest and excite them all. Chief Manuelito advanced, and extending his hand in greeting, said that he had often wished to meet me, the wizard who had beaten the champion marksman of the Navajo tribe.

Several years before I had in the town of Cubero, at the request of Mexican friends, shot a target match with the most renowned marksman of the Navajo tribe, my pistol being pitted against the Navajo's rifle, and had beaten him with a wonderful shot to the discomfiture and distress of a trading band of Indians, who bet on their champion's prowess and lost their goods to the knowing Mexicans.

The chief then requested me to favor them with an exhibition of my skill. I readily assented and directed them to put up a target. They placed a flat rock against the trunk of a pine tree at so great a distance that it was barely distinguishable to the naked eye. I guessed the distance and my shot fell just below the mark. Then I raised the hind sight of my Winchester a notch and the next shot shattered the stone to pieces. At this the Indians went wild. They had thought it impossible for any man to perform this feat of marksmanship, and were most enthusiastic in the profession of their admiration. Gladly would they have adopted me into their tribe as a great chief or medicine man had I wished to ally myself to them. There was the opportunity of a lifetime, but I did not embrace it.

As the sun was now low in the heavens, I advised Don Juan to remain in camp for the night and spoke to Chief Manuelito, expressing my wish to pass through his country unmolested and without delay. The chief assured me of his protection and bade us have no care. We slept soundly that night, a band of Indians guarding our camp and herd under orders of Manuelito, who had become my stanch friend and admirer. The following day we came to the end of the reservation and soon crossed the boundary line of New Mexico into Arizona.

CHAPTER IX.

IN ARIZONA

I left New Mexico with the intention of making Los Angeles in the golden State my future home, and now, thirty years later, I have not reached there yet. Vainly have I tried to break the thraldom of my fate, for I did not know that here I was to meet face to face with the mighty mystery of an ancient cult, the God of a long-forgotten civilization, a psychic power which has ordered my path in life and controlled my actions.

As its servant, at its bidding, I write this, and shall now unfold, and in the course of this narrative give to the world a surprising revelation of the power of ancient Aztec idols, which would be incredible in the light of our twentieth century of Christian civilization if it were not sustained by the evidence of undeniable facts.

Our road led through a hilly country toward the Little Colorado River. In the distance loomed the San Francisco Mountains, extinct craters which had belched fire and lava long, long ago at the birth of Arizona, when the earth was still in the travail of creation. We forded the Little Colorado at Sunset Crossing, a lonely colony, where a few Mormons were the only inhabitants of a vast area of wilderness. We were headed due west toward a mesa rising abruptly from the plateau which we were then traversing. This mesa was again capped by a chain of lofty peaks, one of the Mogollon mountain ranges. We ascended the towering mesa through the difficult Chavez pass, which is named after its discoverer, the noted Mexican, Colonel Francisco Chavez, who may be remembered as a representative in Congress of the United States, for the Territory of New Mexico. A day's heavy toil brought us to the summit of the mesa, which was a beautiful place, but unspeakably lonesome. This wonderful highland is a malpais or lava formation and densely covered with a forest of stately pines and mountain juniper. Strange to say, vegetation thrives incredibly in the rocky lava; a knee-high growth of the most nutritious grama grasses, indigent to this region, rippled in the breeze like waves of a golden sea and we saw numerous signs of deer, antelope, and turkey. Our road, a mere trail, wound over this plateau, which was a veritable impenetrable jungle in places, a part of the great Coconino forest. Think and wonder! An unbroken forest of ten thousand square miles, it is said to be the most extensive woodland on the face of the globe. This trail was the worst road to travel I have seen or expect ever to pass over. The wagons moved as ships tossed on a stormy sea, chuck! chuck! from boulder to boulder, without intermittence. We found delicious spring water about noon and passed a most remarkable place later in the day. This must have been the pit of a volcano. A few steps aside from the road you might lean over the precipice and look straight down into a great, round crater, so deep that it made a person dizzy. At the bottom there was a ranch house, a small lake and a cultivated field, the whole being apparently ten acres in area. I looked straight down on a man who was walking near the house and appeared no larger than a little doll and his dog seemed to be the size of a grasshopper, but we heard the dog bark and heard the cackling of hens quite plainly. On one side of this pit there was a break in the formation, which made this curious place accessible by trail.

We had been advised that we would find a natural tank of rain water in the vicinity of this place and camped there at nightfall. We turned our stock out, but our herders did not find the promised water. Our cook reported that there was not a drop of water in camp, as the spigot of his water tank had been loosened by the roughness of the road and all the water was lost. Now this would have been a matter of small consequence if Don Juan had not been taken ill suddenly. He threw himself on the ground and cried for water. "Agua, por Dios!" (Water, for God's sake) he cried, "or I shall die." "Why, Don Juan," I said, "there is no water here. I advise you to wait till moonrise when the cattle are rested and then leave for the next watering place, which is Beaver Head, at the foot of the mesa; we ought to reach there about ten o'clock to-morrow morning. Surely until then you can endure a little thirst!" "Amiga, I cannot, I am dying," moaned Don Juan, in great distress. As I suspected that he had lost his nerve on the Navajo reservation, I felt greatly annoyed, and when he became frantic in his cries I promised to go down to Beaver Creek to get him a drink of water, for I recalled to mind his little daughter who bid me farewell with these words: "Adios, Senor Americano, I charge you with the care of my padrecito. If you promise me, I know that he will return to me safely."

I set out on my long night-walk, stumbling over rocks and boulders in the darkness. It was a beautiful night, the crisp atmosphere was laden with the fragrant exhalation of the nut pines and junipers and there was not a breath of air stirring. I got down to water at midnight, the time of moonrise, filled my canteen and started on the return trip. Slowly I reascended the steep mesa, and when I reached the summit I sat down on a rock in a thicket of junipers. The moon had now risen above the trees and cast its dim light over an enchanting scene. The sense of utter loneliness, a homesickness, a feeling of premonition, stole over me, and weirdly I sensed the presence of I knew not what. From the shadows spoke an owl, sadly, anxiously, "Hoo, hoo! Where are you? You!" and his mate answered him tenderly, seductively, "Tee, hee! Come to me! Me!"

In the west, far, far away, clustered a range of mountains, spread out like an enormous horse-shoe and in its center arose the form of a solitary hill. In the heavens from the east drifted a white, ragged cloud. The solitary hill seemed to rise high and higher and all the mountains bowed before it. The spectral cloud resolved itself into a terrible vision which enveloped the central hill. Great Heavens! Again I saw the phantom dog and fancied that I heard shrill screams of "Perro, perro, gringo perro!" A crackling noise, a coming shadow, and forward I fell on my face, ever on the alert, ever ready. An unearthly yell and a great body flew over, fierce claws grazing me. Two balls of fire shone in the bush, but my rifle cracked and a great lion fell in its tracks. I expected my companions to meet me soon, coming my way. Instead, I found them, after my all-night's walk, snugly camped where I had left them. Don Juan explained that with God's favor they had found the water soon after I had left them. He said that they had called loud and long after me, but I did not seem to hear.

This day we descended the mesa and entered the valley of the Verde River, one of Arizona's permanent water courses. This valley is cultivated for at least forty miles from its source to where it enters precipitous mountains. We forded the crystal waters of the river at

Camp Verde, an army post, and crossed another range of mountains and several valleys into a comparatively open country, and on the night of a day late in November we camped on Lynx Creek, and were then within a half day's travel of our destination.

CHAPTER X.

AT THE SHRINE OF A "SPHINX OF AZTLAN"

Not a drop of rain had fallen on us since we left the Rio Grande, the days were as summer in a northern climate, but the nights were quite chill, the effect of an altitude of five thousand feet above sea level. The country had lost its appearance of loneliness, for we passed several parties of miners and heard the heavy booming of giant powder at intervals, and from various directions all through the day.

We were joined by a jolly party of miners who were eager for news and camped with us over night. There were three men in this outfit. Keen-looking, hearty old chaps with ruddy faces and gray beards, they looked like men who are continually prospecting for the "main chance." I passed a delightful evening in their company. They said they owned rich silver mines farther up on Lynx Creek, and had come out from town to perform the annual assessment work on their claims, as prescribed by the laws of the United States, in order to hold possession and perfect legal title to the ground. As I was not versed in matters pertaining to the mines, I asked why they did not work their mines continually for the silver. They explained that they could not work to good advantage for lack of transportation facilities which made it very difficult and costly to bring in machinery for developing their prospects into mines. Therefore, until the advent of railroads they chose to perform their annual assessment work only.

Two of these gentlemen were substantial business men and the other was their confidential secretary or affidavit man. It was his duty to make an affidavit before a magistrate that his employers had performed the labor required by law, which is not less than one hundred dollars per claim and incidentally he cooked for the outfit and attended to the horses. Of course, they might have hired mine laborers to do this work, but they said they enjoyed the outing and exercise, especially as this was the time of house cleaning and they were glad to get away from home. "Yes," affirmed the affidavit man, "and so are your wives."

These gentlemen rode horses and carried a supply of provisions on a pack mule. The most conspicuous object of their pack was a keg labelled "dynamite." When the clerk placed this dangerous thing near the fire and sat on it, I became fidgety, but was reassured when subsequently I saw him draw the stopper and fill a bottle labelled "Old Crow" from it. They advised me to go prospecting and gave me much valuable information and kindly offered to sell me a prospecting outfit, "for cash," at their stores.

As we were chatting, I became aware of a delicious, pungent odor, like the perfume of orange blossoms. "Is it possible," said I, astonished, "that there are orange groves in bloom in this vicinity?" The old gentlemen said they did not smell anything wrong, but the clerk jumped to his feet and sniffed the air in the direction of Prescott. "Why, gentlemen," said he, "of course, you cannot smell any further than the blossoms on the tips of your noses, but the young man has a sharp proboscis, he scents the girls. Here comes Dan bound for the Silver Bell Mine with his blooming show." We heard the clatter of hoofs and wheels and saw a large coach pass by, crowded with passengers, mostly ladies. The clerk said that the genial owner of the Silver Bell Mine, who was also the proprietor of a popular resort in town, was going out to pay his miners their monthly wage. "That is it," said one of the merchants, "and to keep the boys from leaving the mine in order to spend their money at his resort in town, he takes his variety show out there. He cannot afford to have his mine shut down just now, as they have struck horn silver, and that is the kind of tin he needs in his business."

These kind old gentlemen cautioned me to keep away from a dark-looking, broken mountain, looming to the north. "That country is no good," they said; "there is nothing but copper there, even the water is poisoned with it." Those were the black hills where there is now the prosperous town of Jerome and one of the great mines of the earth, the famous United Verde Mine, the property of Senator William Clark.

The following day, about noon, we rounded a sharp bend of the road and Fort Whipple and the town of Prescott came into view. A pretty and gratifying sight truly, but imagine my astonishment! Here to the right was the identical mysterious hill which I had seen in that memorable night from the height of the Mogollon mesa and behind it was the black range, the Sierra Prieta, which had formed a part of the encircling horseshoe.

Never in my lifetime have I come to a town where the people were as hospitable and kindly disposed toward strangers as here. It is no wonder that I got no farther, for here the people vied with each other to welcome the wayfarer to the gates of their city. The town was then young and isolated. The inhabitants had come by teams or horseback from as far away as the State of Kansas, where the nearest railway connection was eastward, or from California, via Yuma and Ehrenberg on the Colorado River. Stages and freight teams made regular trips across the arid desert to Ehrenberg. The first settlers of this region came from California in search of gold. They first found it in the sands of the Hassayampa, which is born of mighty Mount Union, the mother of four living streams. From its deathbed in the hot sands of the desert, they traced the precious waters to its source. Gold they found in plenty with hardship and privation. They encountered a band of hostile Indians, and hardest to bear, a loneliness made sufferable only by the illusive phantasies of the golden fever. Their expectations realized, the majority of these pioneers returned to the Golden State and civilization with the burden of their treasure, saying they had not come to Arizona for their health. Now in these present days there comes a throng of people in quest of health solely, and many are they who find its blessing in the sunny and bracing air of this climate, in hot springs and the balmy breath of the fir and juniper of our mountains. I found employment in a mercantile establishment of this little mining town and grew up with the country, as the saying is. I formed new acquaintances and made new friends. Among others, I met William Owen O'Neill. I cannot now remember the exact time or year. Attracted by the light-hearted, cheerful, and dare-devil spirit of this ambitious and cultured young man, I joined a military organization, of which he was then a lieutenant and later the captain, this was Company F of Prescott Grays, National Guard of Arizona. Poor, noble-hearted, generous Buckie—he knew it not, but this was his first step on the path of glory leading to the altar of patriotism whereon he laid his life. It was he who, with a poet's inspiration, first divined the mystery of the mountain which I have before alluded to. He likened this beautiful mound to a sleeping lion who guarded the destinies of the mountain city. Poor friend, his glorious song stirred the dormant life in the metallic veins of the Butte and, wonder of wonders, the sleeping lion awoke, the poet's lay had brought the Sphinx to life—the die of fate was cast and he had sealed his doom! When I read his beautiful poem, I gasped in wonder, for only I on earth fathomed the significance of this revelation. This dream of a poet's fanciful soul, soaring on the wings of Pegasus, was stern reality to me and anxiously I awaited developments. Nor waited I in vain.

The grateful Sphinx showered honor and wealth upon my friend. The generous sportive boy, who cared naught for gold, actually grew rich, for the Sphinx had granted him the most lucrative office in the county, the people made him their sheriff. He rose step by step to the highest place of honor in the community until he became the mayor of Prescott. Not satisfied with this token of its favor, the Sphinx rewarded him in a most extraordinary and convincing manner. By the help of nature, its help-meet, it transformed a great deposit of siliceous limestone into beautiful onyx and painted it in all the colors and after the pattern of the rainbow. This magnificent gift made Captain O'Neill independently rich, but it is a fact that as soon as it passed from his hands, the stone lost in value and no one has since profited from it. I believe that our hero would have risen to the highest position of dignity on earth, the Presidency of the United States, if he had not unwittingly aroused the jealousy of the terrible heathen god. When he chose a wife from the lovely maidens of Prescott, then the vengeful Sphinx laid its sinister plans for his undoing, for it is in the nature of cats, small or great, to be exceedingly jealous. The furious idol remembered the people of a long forgotten race, its loyal subjects, who had reared and worshiped it, inconceivably long ago, when the Grand Canyon of Arizona was but a tiny ravine and before icy avalanches had ground the rocks at the Dells into boulders. It remembered the descendants of its subjects, the Aztec Indians. It remembered how the Spaniards had cruelly broken the Aztec nation. Through the subtle influence of psychic forces, it stirred up a passion of hate for Spain in the hearts of the people of the United States, and it fostered the awful spirit of strife, and at the right moment it let loose the dogs of war. One convulsive touch of its rocky claws on the hidden currents coursing in earth's veins and an evil spark fired the fatal mine under the battleship Maine, in the harbor of Havana.

"Is this possible; can this be true?" If not, why is it that at the call to arms, even before the nation rallied from the shock of the cowardly deed which sacrificed the lives of inoffensive sailors — why is it, I say, that from under the very paws of the Sphinx, so far away in Arizona — and at the call of Captain O'Neill, the noble mayor of Prescott, there arose the first contingent of fighting volunteers in our war with Spain? The inexorable Sphinx had resolved to grant to our beloved and honored friend its last and most exalted gift, a hero's death on the field of battle. It has graven the name of Prescott, the city of the Sphinx, on scrolls of everlasting fame, as the town which rallied first to the call of the President and as the only town which gave the life of its mayor, its first, its most honored citizen, to the nation.

On the isle of Cuba, in the battle of San Juan Hill, fell the gallant Captain William Owen O'Neill of the regiment of Rough Riders. Peace to his ashes!

I have been told the circumstances surrounding his death by friends, who were soldiers of his company. They were lying under cover behind every available shelter to dodge a hailstorm of Mauser bullets, awaiting the order to advance. Captain O'Neill exposed himself and was instantly killed. How could he avoid it? How could it have been otherwise? What can keep an Irishman down in the ditch when bullets are flying in air, "murmuring dirges" and "shells are shrieking requiems?" You may readily imagine an Irishman on the firing line, poking his head above the ground, exclaiming: "Did yez see that? And where did that Dago pill come from now? Shure it spoke Spanish, but it did not hit me at all, at all, Begorra!"

The activity of the Sphinx ended not with the battle of San Juan Hill, for it cast the luster of its glorious power on the gallant Lieutenant Colonel of the famous regiment of Rough Riders, Theodore Roosevelt, and on him it conferred in time the greatest honor to be achieved on earth, it made him President of the United States of

America. Not knowing it, perhaps, he still is at the time of this writing in the sphere of influence and in the power of the Sphinx and is doing its bidding. Else why should he, as is well known, favor the jointure of New Mexico and Arizona into one State? Surely the loyal subjects of the Sphinx, the Pueblo Indians of Aztec blood, live mostly in New Mexico, and the cunning idol plans to deliver them out of the hands of the Spanish Mexicans, and place them under the protection and care of the Americans of Arizona, knowing full well that the Anglo-Saxon blood will rule.

Every miner and prospector of Arizona knows that there have been, and are found to this day nuggets of pure gold and silver on the summit of barren hills, in localities and under geological conditions which are not to be reckoned as possible natural phenomena. Whence came the golden nuggets on the summit of Rich Hill at Weaver, where a party of men gathered two hundred thousand dollars worth in a week's time? Whence came the isolated great chunk of silver at Turkey Creek, valued at many thousands? The wisest professor of geology and expert of mines cannot explain it. This, I say, is the gold and silver from ornaments employed in temples of the idols of ancient races, who lived unthinkable thousands of years ago. The very stones of their temples have crumbled and been decomposed, but the precious metal has been formed into nuggets, according to the natural laws of molecular attraction, and under the impulse of gravity and in obedience to the laws of affinity of matter.

People from Prescott in their rambles in the vicinity of Thumb Butte have probably noticed a slag pile as comes from a furnace. I have heard them theorize and argue on the question of its origin or use, as there is not a sign of ore in existence thereabouts to indicate a smelting furnace. I say this was an altar erected I by the ancient worshipers to their idol, the Sphinx. Before it stood the awful sacrificial stone, whereon quivered the bodies of victims while priests tore open their breasts and offered their throbbing hearts in the sacred fire on the altar, a sacrifice to their cruel god. Many prospectors have undoubtedly traced a blood red vein of rock coursing from this place toward Willow Creek—a valuable lode of cinnabar, they must have thought. If they had tested the ore for quicksilver, they would have received discouraging results. Porphyry stained with an unknown petrified substance and without a trace of metal invariably read the analytical assays.

This is the innocent, petrified blood of victims which stained a ledge of porphyry when it ran down the mountain side in torrents, an awful sacrifice to the ancient idols of lust and ignorance. A kindly warning to you, fellow-prospectors and miners, who delve in the vitals of Mother Earth! Beware Thumb Butte, beware the district of the Sphinx! Have a care, for you know not what you may encounter in this mystic neighborhood! Shun strange gods and set up no idols in your hearts, as you value the salvation of your souls. But if your mine lies in this district, be fearful not to excite the anger of the gnomes of the mountain. Charge lightly, lest you blast the bottom out of your mine. Disturb not the slumber of the spirits of the hills lest they throw a horse into the shaft and push your pay-ore down a thousand feet.

Now, I who am what I am, a servant of the Sphinx, have erected the shrine of my household gods in the beautiful town, which lies in its shadow and is held in its paw. Even now is the Sphinx weaving on the web of my destiny. I hope I may be spared the cumbersome burden of the wealth of a Rockefeller, who is said to possess a billion dollars for every hair on his head. One thousandth part of his wealth would suffice to reward me amply.

I received a message in a dream, in a vision of the night, a promise from the Sphinx. I fancied that I was on Lynx Creek, sitting on the windlass at the shaft of my silver mine. This mine is within a mile of the place where we had camped and met the party of miners. I had worked the mine with profit until I met, through no fault of mine, with a fault in the mine and encountered a horse in the formation which faulted the ground in such a manner as to interrupt the pay chute and to make further work unprofitable.

While I sat there, lighting my pipe and blessing my luck, I saw a black tomcat come along and jump my claim. As I have always detested claim jumpers, I threw a rock at him and with an uncanny mee-ow and bristling tail he disappeared down the mine. When I went to the spot where he had scratched, after the fashion of cats, probably preparing to build his location monument and place his notice, I was thunderstruck to see that the rock I had thrown at him had been transformed into a chunk of pure gold. Surely where that cat jumped into the mine, there lies a bonanza, there shall I sink to the water level.

From the time of my youth have I always possessed great bodily strength and physical endurance, combined with good health, and now, I am, if anything, stronger in body than ever and I am blessed with the identical passions and thoughts I harbored in the days of my youth. To me this signifies that my life's real task is now beginning, the Sphinx is fitting me for glorious work. What and where, I care not; but ambitious hope leads me on, past wealth and power to visions of a temple of divine, pictorial art. Fain would I guide my light, frivolous thoughts long enough into the calm channels of serious reflection to bid you, my kind readers, a dignified farewell and express the sincere hope that, when we have prospected life's mortal vein to the end of time and our souls soar on the last blast of Gabriel's trumpet to shining sands on shores of bliss eternal.

AN UNCANNY STONE.

(A sequel to the last chapter of "Wooed by a Sphinx of Astlan."')

"Gigantic shadows, dancing in the twilight
Fade with the sun's last golden ray.
On quivering bat-wings, sad and silent,
Flits darkness—night pursuing day.
Hark! as the twelfth hour sounds its knell
At midnight, tolls a whimpering bell
When yawning graves profane their secrecy.
Ghosts stalk in dreamland haunting memory
And spectral visions of departed friends arise
Who freed of sin, that fetter of mortality,
With Angels in their kingdom of Eternal Life
Grace Heaven's choir of harmony."

The third day of July A. D. 1907 was a gala-day for the citizens of Prescott, a historic date for Arizona, as then our governor, in behalf of the territory, formally accepted an equestrian statue from its sculptor.

This monument which commemorates our war with Spain had been erected on the public plaza of Prescott in honor of "Roosevelt's Rough Riders," the first regiment of United States Volunteer cavalry.

A master-piece of modern art the statue breathes life and action in the perfection of its every detail, representing a Rough Rider who is about to draw his weapon while reining his terrified horse as it rears in a last lunge. This is indicated by the steed's gaping mouth, distended nostrils, the bent knees, knotted chords and veins of its neck and body.

The expression of a noble beast's agony is rendered in so life-like a manner that its protruding eyes seem to glaze into the awful stare of death, and instinctively the spectator listens for the stifled whimper and whinnying screams of a wounded creature.

Borglum's splendid statuary, this heroic cast of bronze which so faithfully portrays the destiny of a dumb animal, man's most useful and willing slave, always ready to share its master's fate, even unto death—to my mind is a most eloquent, if silent, argument against all warfare.

But the glory of the monument is its pedestal.

A solid stone, a bed-rock from the cradle of the idol-mountain it was contributed by nature to the memory of one of its noblemen, "Captain William Owen O'Neill," who crowned his life with immortality, suffering a soldier's death.

During the storming of San Juan Hill to anxious friends imploring him not recklessly to expose himself, with smiling lips he gave this message of death's Angel, that mysterious oracle of a Sphinx which from the gaze of mortals veils their ordained doom: "Comrades, sergeant! I thank you for your kindly warning—fear not for me, the Spanish bullet that could kill me is not molded!"—when instantly he fell struck dead—not by a "Spanish" bullet—"no!" but by the bullet fired from a Mauser rifle, "not made in Spain." Not an ordinary stone this Arizona granite rock is entitled to highest honors among the stones of the earth.

By none outclassed in witchery it ranks equally in fame with the Blarneystone of Ireland; old Plymouth Rock does not compare with it, for that derives its prestige only from "Mayflower pilgrims" who accidentally landing at its base merely stepped over it.

Proudly our Arizona stone bears a most precious burden—the tribute of a people who in exalting patriotism honor themselves.

Originally an archaean sea-bottom rock this stone lay submerged in the ocean until during the Jurassic Period, under the lateral pressure of a cooling earthcrust the table-lands and mountain-chains of Arizona rose from the seas.

Then it slumbered through several epochs of geology, representing many millions of years in the bosom of earth, the mother, until at the beginning of the psychozoic era, through erosion or the action of atmospheric influences and nature's chemistry it came to the surface; uncovered and freed from all superimposed stratified rock.

It saw the light of day long before the advent of primitive man; but the giant-flora and fauna of pre-historic time had developed, flourished and vanished while it rested under ground.

Contrary to the habit of rolling stones which gather no moss, this Arizona stone accumulated much, for when it had reached its assigned site on the plaza of Prescott it had become a very valuable, expensive rock.

When first I saw it, this fearful Aztec juggernaut was within a half mile of its destination. Slowly it crawled along, threatening destruction to everything in its path, and in the course of a week had arrived at the Granite-creek bridge.

It moved by main strength and brute force employing men and horses after the custom of the ancients when more than thirty-seven hundred years ago King Menes, son of Cham reigned in Egypt, who albeit surnamed Mizrain the Laggard, yet was the first king of the first dynasty of the children of the sun.

When I saw the direction from whence the stone had come I feared that disaster would overwhelm our town and unfortunately was I not mistaken.

At the bridge the stone gave the first manifestation of its unholy heathen power when it balked, defying modern civilization and through sorcery or in other unhallowed ways contrived to interfere with the public electric traction service, paralyzing the traffic so effectively that every street car in the town was stopped; not merely a few hours, but for days.

Like that colossus of strength and wisdom, the elephant which refuses to pass over a bridge until satisfied that this will uphold its weight, the cunning stone did not budge another inch until the bridge had been braced with many timbers.

As foreseen by me this uncanny rock was sent by the Idol of the mountain, the "Sphinx of Aztlan," to cast a hoodoo, an evil spell over the monument.

It caused dissension among the people and confused their minds into rendering abnormal criticisms, making them indulge in eccentric vagaries and speculations on the artistic and intrinsic value of the monument. Some persons guessed at the value of the metal contained in the statue, while others reckoned the cost of the horse or that of the rider's accoutrements.

However, of thousands of admiring and delighted spectators none shared an exactly like opinion except in this, that the statue bore no individual resemblance; but that also was contradicted by a young lady whom I heard exclaim: "Girls, surely that looks like Buckie O'Neill, but in love and war men are not themselves!" "How do I know? Oh, mamma said so!"

During the ceremony of unveiling the monument a dark, ragged storm cloud hung over the Aztec mountain, fast overcasting the sky. Thousands of people strained their eyes and held their breath in the glad anticipation of seeing the features of their lamented friend, Prescott's honored mayor, immortalized in bronze. When after moments of anxious suspense the veil which draped the statue parted and fell to earth, the sun's rays pierced the clouds, while deafening cheers rent the air. I thought I heard a weird, faint cry, an echo from the past—but cannons boomed, drums crashed as a military band rendered its patriotic airs.

And we saw—not the familiar, fine features of our soldier hero, so strikingly portrayed by a famed artist and molded into exact, lifelike resemblance, but instead we beheld an unknown visage—a type, merely the semblance of a "Rough Rider," its rigid gaze riveted on the Idol-mountain, forever enthralled by the Sphinx.

> In nineteen hundred seven, on the third day of July
> With shining mien and naming sword earthward St. Michael came
> To save—ever auspicious be the blessed day—
> From blighting heathen guile a Christian hero's fame
> The while, breathless with awe, solemn the people gazed
> And rhetoric's inspired flame on Aztlan's altar blazed.
> Adore the Saints, behold a miracle Divine!
> Hallowed, our Saviour, be Thy Name
> And Heaven's glory thine!

Of idol-worship now has vanished every trace
In deepest crevice and highest place
On mesa, butte and mountain-face;
From the Grand Canyon's somber shade
The sun-scorched desert, the dripping glade
And sunken crater of Stoneman's Lake.
The "Casa Grande," a home of ancient race—
A ruin now—is haunted by Montezuma's wraith.
In Montezuma's castle, crumbling from roof to base
The winds and rain of heaven ghosts of the past now chase.

Where erstwhile the Great Spirit's children dwelt
Forever hushed is the papoose's wail, and stilled the squaw's
low-crooning lilt.
No longer shimmers starlight from eyes of savage maids
Worshippers of the fire and sun, poor dwellers of the caves—
The sisters of the deer and lo, shy startled fawns of Aztec
race
Or coy ancestral dams of moon-eyed Toltec doe.
Now Verde witches bathe in Montezuma's well
And over its crystal waters the tourists cast their spell.

Rejoice! To Arizona has the Saviour vouchsafed His Grace
For our Salvation Army lass teaches true Gospel faith:
"Be saved this night, poor sinner, repent, the hour is late!
Salvation is in store for thee, brother do not delay
As fleeting time and sudden death for no man ever wait!"
"Praise God!" the lassie's war-cry is, the keynote of her song.
To the tune of "Annie Roonie" and kindred fervid lay
With mandolin and banjo, marching in bold array
The devil's strongholds storming, battling to victory—
With banners flying, the tambourine and drum
Forever has she silenced the shamans vile tom-tom.
All Fetish Spirit-medicine she has tabooed, banished away
Except bourbon and rye, sour-mash, hand-made
And copper-distilled, licensed, taxed and gauged,
Then stored in bond to ripen, mellow, age.

God bless the Army, rank and file who fight our souls to
save!
Modern disciples of the Son of Man, true followers of Christ,
They work by day, then preach and pray and pound their
drum at night.

L'ENVOY.

Farewell, this ends my rhyming, submitted at its worth.
Lest I forget—pride goes before the fall, on earth
And exceeding fine if slowly, grind the mills of angry gods—
The muses' steed, a versifying bronco had I caught
And recklessly I rode; but fast as thought
Fate overtook me when Pegasus bucked me off.
Sorely distressed I hear a satyr's mocking laugh
As on my laurels resting, on my seat of honor cast
And thanking you for kind attention now your indulgent
censure ask.

THE BIRTH OF ARIZONA. (AN ALLEGORICAL TALE.)

On the summit of a mountain I staked my claim; in the shade of a balsam-spruce I built my hut.

When the south wind that rises on the desert climbs to the mountain's ridge and rustling among silvery needles, rattles the cones on boughs and twigs—the tree-giant whispers with resinous breath, bemoaning the fate of a prehistoric civilization, and lisps of the mystery and romance of a humanity long extinct, mourning for races forgotten and vanished.

Alone—unrivaled in her weird, wild grandeur stands Arizona where spiry rock-ribbed giants stab an emerald, opal-tinted sky, and terraced mesas of wondrous amber hue form natural stairways, that grandly wrought were carved step after step, through successive epochs of erosion, affording thus an easy ascent to the rugged profile of this land of the Western Hemisphere. All this is of historic record in stony cypher of geology indelibly engraved by time on the rocky walls of deepest canyons, as traceable from the primordial archaean to our present era, the age of man.

In tremor-spasms of terrestrial creation, 'midst chaotic fiery turmoil of volcanos, out of the depth of globe-encircling waters, from the womb of Universe—Eternity—came the Almighty Word, and then was born fair Arizona.

Fraught with golden prophecy was her horoscope, cast by fate's oracle for her birthday fell under the sign of the scorpion when in the path of planets Venus contended with the Earth for first place of ascendency to the second house of the heavens.

High above the tidal wave rose Arizona, as fleecy clouds float in the rays of Apollo's sun-torch when at eventide his flaming chariot plunges into unfathomed depths of the Pacific Ocean.

With her first breath this daughter of Columbia, born of gods, clamored for aid. Neptune was first among the planets to heed the plaintive cry and held her to his breast, with fond caresses.

The grandest canyon on the face of earth with flowing streams and limpid crystals he gave her as a birthday present.

These crystals rare are famed as Arizona diamonds now.

Bright, lovely Venus, the sister of Earth, a shining planet, gave the ruby-red garnet, her pledge of love and Arizona hid it in her bosom. There shall you find it, if worthy so you be, in the hearts of happy maidens.

Saturn gave her his ring of amethysts and Uranus the greenish malachite, of buoyant hope the emblem. This, in time, was changed to copper, the king of all commercial metals.

Mars gave the bloodstone. From it came soldiers bold, heroes who fought Apaches and the Spaniard.

The winged Mercury on passing tossed her two stones, most precious; the lodestone and a Blackstone. The lodestone was a stone of grit. When Arizona placed it in her crib thence came the lucky prospector who sinks his shafts through earth and rock in search of mineral treasure.

Then opened she the Blackstone and lo, from it arose the men of eloquence who aided by retainers fight keenly in continued terms for order, law and justice with weapons that are mightier than the sword which giveth glory, eternal rest and immortality to heroes only whom it smiteth.

Behold, a shadow now fell on the Earth and as a serpent coils and creeping stretches forth its slimy length, it came apace.

Foreboding evil it announced the knight-errant of never-ending space, a wicked comet. To Arizona gave he playthings many: the rattlesnake, hairy tarantelas and stinging scorpions, horned toads and centipedes, a scented hydrophobia-cat, the Gila monster, a Mexican and the Apache; also a thorny cactus plant.

Anon the tricky Hassayampa rose from his source. On mischief bent he overflowed his bed, teasing the infant Arizona. He worried her, poor dearie—dear till she shed tears and nature adding to the gush of waters there flowed a brackish stream away; now named Saltriver and on its banks nested the Phoenix.

From Elysium in his chariot descended then the sungod to nurse his infant daughter. He dried the Hassayampa's bed in the hot desert sand and where man-like, incautiously he scorched the hem of Arizona's dress—where now lies Yuma—there the temperature rose ten degrees hotter than hades; but luckily since then it has cooled off as much.

The happy maiden smiled with joy as Apollo kissed her long and often. He took the turquoise from the skies, an emblem of unfaltering faith. It and a lock of shining hair he gave her. That hid she in her rocky bed where it became gold of the mint; the filthy lucre of unworthiness and avarice, a blessing when in charity bestowed; a boon as the reward of honest labor!

With lengthening shadows Luna, night's gentle goddess came, a full mile nearer to Arizona than to other lands beaming her softest rays over the sleeping child. Under the lunar kisses woke Arizona and stored the moonshine in her gown. That nature has transformed to silver; serving the poor man as his needed coin.

In sadness waned the moon, for caught between the horns of a dilemma she had no wealth left to endow the infant with. Intemperate habits had the goddess always, was often full and now reduced to her last quarter, but that was waning fast and her man's shadow also growing less. Her semi-transparent stone, alas! had given she long since to California, but this proudest of all daughters of the seas did not appreciate the kindly gift. She cast it on the white sands of her beaches where it is gathered by the thankful tourist who shouts exultantly, delighted with his find:

> The moonstone, climate, atmosphere,
> The only things free-gratis here—
> Eureka!
> I have found!

A ROYAL FIASCO.

(HISTORICAL ANECDOTES.)

A village on the coast of northern Germany, where the Elbe flows into the North Sea, was my birthplace, its parsonage, my childhood's home.

Two great earth-dikes which sheltered our village from fierce southwesterly gales were the only barrier standing between untold thousands of lives and watery graves, for the coasts of Holland and northern Germany are below the level of high tides.

It is known that through inundations caused by breaks in these levees, occurring as late as the tenth and eleventh centuries of our era more than three hundred thousand persons with all their domestic cattle were drowned over night.

These dikes which extend for many miles along the banks of the river were erected by the systematic herculean toil of generations of our ancestors.

According to a popular tradition it was Rolof, the dwarf, a thrall of Vulcan, who taught my forefathers the art of forging tools from iron ore, enabling them to battle successfully against the might of Neptune.

They blunted the angry sea-god's trident with their plows and shovels and repulsed him at the very threshold of his element, stemming the inroads of hungry seas with their stupendous handiwork which still stands intact, an imposing monument to the memory of my forebears, being their children's children's most precious inheritance.

On the soil which my ancestors reclaimed from the sea they founded their homes and sowed grasses and cereals.

But ere long a dire calamity came over the land, for at the command of the revengeful Neptune his mermaids spewed sea-foam into the river's fresh water addling it with their fish-tails into a nasty brine.

Luckily the good dwarf who in his youth had served his term of apprenticeship at the court of King Gambrinus and was therefore master of the noble craft of brewing kindly taught my forefathers to brew a foaming draught from the malt of barleycorn, which thereafter they drank instead of water.

And now all seafaring men who navigate the river Elbe between Cuxhaven and Hamburg are still troubled with a tremendous thirst which nothing but foaming lager beer may quench.

The founding of the village's church dates from the conversion of Saxon tribes who inhabited that country. The chapel's original walls were built of rock, but its newer part was constructed of brick-work during the fourteenth century.

Our domicile, the parsonage, although not quite as ancient, was a very picturesque ruin with its moss-covered roof of thatched straw, under which a flock of sparrows made their homes; but a modern building, how prosaic-looking it might be, or deficient in uniqueness and the charm of its surroundings, would undeniably have made a better, more sanitary and comfortable residence.

Mother, at least, thought this when father landed her, his blushing bride at the ancient parsonage in a rain storm which compelled them to retire for the night under the shelter of an umbrella; and thus the honeymoon of their married life waxed with uncommon hardship.

Later the old leaky house received a tile roof, part of it was removed and with it the room where first I saw the light of day.

That was a cold day for father indeed, as there was another mouth to be fed then, a very serious problem for a poor parson to solve.

When my aunt remarked that I looked like a "monk" father eyed me thoughtfully, saying: "Perhaps there is something to Darwin's theory after all," but mother took me to her arms, withering her sister with scornful glances of her flashing eyes. "Certainly does he look like a monk, the poor little tiddledee-diddy darling," she said; "what else would you expect of him, being the son of a preacher and a descendant of priests?"

On a certain fateful summer day when assembled at dinner we heard the rumble of wheels as an imperial post-chaise hove into view, lumbering lazily past the parsonage.

The postillion's horn sounded a letter-call and my sisters rushed out, racing over our lawn to the gate, in order to take the message. They returned with a large envelope bearing great official seals, both girls struggling for its possession and fighting like cats for the privilege of carrying the precious document. Mother's face was wreathed in smiles of ecstacy.

"Your salary, papa," she whispered, but father was very solemn. "No, dear, it is not due," he answered. He took the missive from my sister's hands and turned it over and over, guessing at its contents until mother who was favored with more of that quality which is commonly called "presence of mind" urged him to open it, and see.

An ashen pallor spread over father's countenance, the letter dropped from his hand and he would have fallen if mother had not caught him in her arms. She grabbed the evil message, slipping it into the bosom of her gown, where it could do no further harm.

Then she guided father's faltering steps to the sanctity of his studio, where he wrote his sermons and closed the door.

My sisters availed themselves of the opportunity to make a raid on mother's pantry, but I, poor little innocent, waited in the corridor for mother's return, dreading to hear the worst. I heard my dear father groan aloud and bemoan his fate and listened to mother's soothing sympathetic words as she begged father to be calm and bear it like a man and a Christian.

When at last mother came out I flew to her. She took me to her arms, kissing my tear-stained face.

"Poor little boy," she said, "cheer up and you shall have a big cookie, don't you cry!"

"Oh, mamma," I faltered, "will papa die?"

"No, sonny, that he won't," said she with a determined glint of her eyes and a twitching of the corners of her mouth, "for I won't let him; but he does suffer anguish!"

"Oh, tell me, mamma, what misfortune has befallen us," I cried.

"It is very sad," said mother. "Your father, who is the finest speaker in the country, has been commanded by a worshipful senate and most honorable civic corporation of the Free City of Hamburg to appear before the visiting king in full dress, and officiate as orator of the day at a reception to be tendered his majesty by our city"—here mother broke down completely, overwhelmed by grief and wept copiously into her handkerchief.

"Oh, oh," I wailed, "do say it, mamma!"

"And—and your father has no coat!" she sobbed. "Poor man, he fears disgrace and dreads the loss of preferment and of a royal decoration, perhaps. He will have to feign sickness as an excuse for his absence; but I hope he realizes now how degraded and unhappy I must feel with my last year's gowns and made-over millinery—and your poor sister's ancient bonnets, I dare not look at them any longer!"

"But papa has a coat," I said, "a royal Prince Albert!"

"True," answered mother, "but it has no swallow's tails!"

"A Prince Albert has no swallow-tails?" I gasped wonderingly; "but it has great, long tails, surely!"

"Oh, now I see," an idea flashing through my mind; "it has cocktails, has it, mamma, and it can't swallow them, can it, mamma?"

"Oh my, oh my!" screamed mother, "you are the funniest little chap to ask me questions. Go, ask pussy!"

Then I went into the back yard to interview my favorite playmate, our big, black tomcat, and aroused him from his cat nap. But he blinked sleepily only, saying nothing.

However, speech was not to be denied me in that manner, for I held the combination which unlocks the portals of silence. I gave the handle a double twist and he spat and spluttered: "Sh—sh—sht—t—t!"

As may be imagined, my father passed a sleepless night in the solitude of his studio. He wrestled with a host of demons and made a good fight of it; for finally in the small hours of morning he overcame the evil spirit of worldly ambition and with true Christian humility, his soul purified by vanquished temptation, resigned himself unreservedly, good man that he was, to the mandate of a cruel fate. He began to write his sermon for the Sabbath, and being spiritually chastened and battle-sore, naturally his thoughts dwelt on melancholy topics. Therefore, he took the text of his sermon from the Lamentations of Jeremiah, chapter 3, v. I:

"I am the man that hath seen affliction by the rod of His wrath."

It may be stated here that on the next Sabbath, from "firstly" to "seventhly" for two long hours father pondered over the uncertainties of earthly life, and that on this occasion he delivered the most effective sermon of his pastoral career.

When father had written his sermon he resumed work on an unfinished volume of historical sketches which he prepared for future publication.

Meantime mother, who was busy with a pleasanter task was correspondingly cheerful. She altered father's "Prince Albert" into a stately full-dress coat, ripping up its waist-seams, and pinned back the skirts of the coat into the proper claw-hammer shape.

Then she took that other garment which goes with the long waistcoat and the full-dress coat of a courtier's suit, in hand.

This article had not been mentioned before by anyone, as there was a goodly supply of it known to be in mother's wardrobe. Deftly cutting the lace away, a few inches above the knees she placed some mother-of-pearl buttons and bows of ribbons and with few stitches fashioned a beautiful pair of courtier's small clothes, or knickerbockers, for father's use.

Father had begun a description of the battle of Waterloo, for nothing so touched a responsive chord in his mind as the recording of a most fearful catastrophe, the direst calamity known to history, nor served as well to alleviate by comparison his mind's distress and mortification.

Just as he wrote the sentence, "Alas for Napoleon, here set his lucky star; not only was his misfortune repeated, but also his final downfall accomplished when Blucher's tardy cavalry appeared on the field, turning the tide of battle in favor of the British"—in came mother with happy, triumphant laughter, unfolding and flaunting to the breeze the so anxiously wished-for full-dress suit.

"Julia, darling, you have saved the day, oh you are so clever," shouted father, joyfully embracing her; "but I say!" he exclaimed in startled surprise, "where on earth did you get this—er—trousseau? Do you really think I shall need those?"

"Yes, indeed you shall, dearest, when you are going to court," replied mother. "Here you have everything needed except the silken hose which you must buy."

"But you have a plenty of long-limbed stockings," said father, wrinkling his brow.

"My good man, look here now!" answered mother, bristling, "well enough you know that all my stockings are very old and holey!"

"Oh, darn them!" growled father testily.

"Wilhelm, do you wish the king to see my stockings then?" cried mamma, angrily.

"But, my dear, you know that he can't see, as he is stone-blind," said father.

"So he is, Wilhelm, and for that very reason he could not find the throne of England," snapped mother, "but never was he blind as you to his queenly wife's unfashionable appearance, nor was he ever deaf to her demands for something decent to wear!"

And mother, as always when it came to ultimate extremes, finally gained her point, for father loved her dearly and dared not deny her.

On the following day arrived the king, for whose reception our township had made grand preparations. Festoons of evergreen decorated the roadway from the parsonage to the opposite house, and mother and my sisters were stationed at our gate with an abundance of roses to strew in the king's path.

From the steeple pealed the chimes, heralding his majesty's arrival. He traveled in an open landau, which was drawn by six milk-white Arabian steeds and surrounded by a select escort of young men who were his subjects and served as his guard of honor.

They wore scarfs of the royal colors over breasts and shoulders.

A courtier sat on either side of the king for the purpose of advising him and to direct his movements.

Poor man, he turned his sightless white eyes on us, bowing to the ladies in acknowledgment of their curtesies and roses.

This king was very unlike his royal namesake predecessors, as he was pitied by everyone and not envied or hated. I must confess to having been sorely disappointed with this sight of royalty, for I thought a king must be an extraordinary being, expecting to see a double-header, as kings and queens are pictured on playing cards, the kings holding scepters in their left hands and bearing a ball with their right, but I saluted and shouted as everyone else did, and when my sisters pelted the royal equipage with their roses I shied my cap at his majesty, at which the people who saw this laughed as loudly as they dared in the presence of a king. I expected also to see a military display, but there were no soldiers present, because the king traveled "incognito," which means that it was forbidden to reveal his royal identity. He was supposed to be a plain nobleman merely, "Herr von Beerstein" for instance.

But a king, who is human after all, may wish to enjoy himself as others do and desire to associate occasionally with ordinary people. So "Herr von Beerstein" goes to a beer garden in quest of a pleasing companion who is readily found, for he has money to burn and invests it freely.

An obliging bar-maid introduces him to her lovely cousin and they retire to a lonely seat in the most secluded spot of the garden.

"Herr von Beerstein" now places his heart and purse in the keeping of his gentle companion, who calls directly for "zwei beers."

Now follows a repetition of the old, old legend that yet is always new and ever recurring in the romance of mutual love on sight, two hearts beating as one and in the love that laughs at locksmiths, but as the course of true love seldom runs smooth, now with the maiden's oft repeated calls for "lager" "Herr von Beerstein" grows by stages sentimental, incautious and then so reckless that "presto!" before he is aware of any danger to himself he has stopped Cupid's fatal dart with his royal personal circumference. Maddened with pain he exhibits symptoms of a most violent passion and becomes very aggressive. But the cunning maid appeals to the protecting presence of Fritz, the waiter, with other calls for beer, whispering in the ear of her love-lorn swain: "Nine, mine lieber Herr von Beerstein, ven you has married me once alretty, nicht wahr? Ach vas, den shall you kiss me yet some more, yaw!"

Thus she tantalizes the poor man until he becomes desperate under the strain of an unrequited love and as a last resort he places his hand over his heart, bares the bosom of his shirt and exposes the insignia of royalty, flashing the sovereign's star before her eyes. Humbly, overcome with shame and remorse at the thought of having trifled with her king's affections, and prompted by her pitiful exaggerated notion of loyalty the poor thing kneels before his majesty, craving his pardon.

With royal hands the king uplifts her, graciously kissing her rosebud mouth and when she says: "Your majesty's slightest wish is a command to me, your servant!" and is about to surrender her loveliness to Cupid's forces and temporarily lose her heart, but her soul forever—in the very nick of time comes her guardian-angel to the rescue.

When she, poor little gray dove, lies trembling in the royal falcon's talons a head rises up and peeps over the fence, for the royal star has been seen through a crack between the boards, its knowing, sly grin passing into the lusty shout:

"Heil dem koenig, hoch, hoch!"

An excited crowd rushes from all directions, cheering: "Ein, zwei, drei, hurrah!" while a constable places the damsel under arrest, charging her with lese majeste. When, however, his majesty intercedes most graciously the your lady is promptly released, and restored to freedom.

But the constable's fee that she must pay—in earthly power, not even a king can save her from it, for that is a "trinkgeld" and she pays it from the royal purse.

On the evening of the king's arrival I accompanied my father to the castle where the reception royal took place. There were no ladies present on this occasion. The king was, as has been said, totally blind, but indulged in the curious habit of feigning to have an unimpaired eye sight and pretended to admire scenic objects which had been pointed out to him beforehand as though he really saw them, carrying out this illusion to the extent of ridiculousness. It is said that at a hunt-meet a courtier incurred his royal displeasure through these incautious words: "Sire, you shot this hare from a next to impossible distance, condescend to feel how fat it is!"

As the poor man failed to say "See how fat," he fell promptly into disfavor, which is equivalent to being blacklisted in our country.

The king's general behaviour suggests that he deemed his blindness not merely to be a most regrettable misfortune, but that he regarded it as a deserved culpable affliction.

When a small boy I was told that he lost his eyesight through an act of charity. He drew a purse from his pocket, intending to give a beggar an aim when his horse shied violently, causing the steel-beaded tassels of the purse to injure his eyes.

Later, as I grew older, I heard a different tale:

The king as a student, then being crown-prince of the realm, found pleasure in looking at the wine which was red, and at a pair of eyes that were blue and shone like heavenly stars, oh so gently and tenderly! But he looked, alas, once too often—into eyes that blazed with lurid flames of hate and fury—the terrible eyes of the green-eyed monster. There came a flash as of lightning with a loud report and he saw stars that fell fiercely fast until they vanished under a cloud of awful gloom in the hopeless despair of perpetual night; but the glorious luminous star of day for him shone not again, nevermore, on earth! To this day I know not which version tells the truth.

The castle's grand hall was overflowing with people. I followed in the wake of father, who had fallen into line, advancing gradually toward the august presence of a crowned king. Nervously father awaited his turn to bask for one anxious moment in the sunshine of royal favor and touch a king's hand.

I slipped away unperceived to the kitchen, knowing well the premises of this fine old castle which was kept in good repair by the city of Hamburg, its present owner. It had been won by conquest of arms in 1394 A.D. from the noble family "Von Lappe."

The principal occupation of these knights was the waylaying and robbing of merchants; but the wrecking of ships was their favorite, most profitable pastime.

The kitchen was in the basement of the castle and great in size, its floor paved with slabs of stone, the walls and ceilings were paneled in oak. On one side of the room were stone-hearths with blazing fires, over which hung pots and brazen kettles. Game and meats broiled on spits, there being no cook-stoves in those days. Heavy doors, strapped with great wrought iron hinges and studded with ornamental scroll-work led into pantries and cellars.

The place swarmed with liveried servants and cooks; also the king had brought his "chef de cuisine and own butler. The latter, a lordly Englishman, was a grand, haughty person who superintended the extravagant preparations for the entertainment of royalty.

A maid conducted me to a corner where I was out of harm's way and regaled me with delicacies when the courses were served, oh it was fine! The chef prepared certain dishes for the king and I saw the butler taste of the viands that were placed on crown-marked dishes of porcelain and gold. He also tasted the king's wine.

When at last I grew sleepy, kind maids arranged a couch of snowy linen for me, and I slept until the banquet royal was over when the guests returned to their homes.

But me lord, the butler, eyed me with questioning curiosity.

"Aw me lad, h'and where did your father get 'is blooming costume?" he asked.

"Mother supplied it, good sir," I answered.

"Hi say, me lad," he laughed, "your mother h'is a grand lydie, you tike me word for h'it; h'in h'England they would decorate that suit with the h'order h'of the garter!"

"Honi soit, qui mal y pense!" I lisped.

A MAID OF YAVAPAI.

To S. M. H.
(AN IDYLLIC SKETCH.)

People from every land sojourn in Arizona.

From the Atlantic's sandy coasts, the icy shores of crystal lakes, from turbid miasmatic swamps—east, north and south, they come.

Over mountain, canyon and gulch they roam, prospecting nature's grandest wonders.

But the purest gold on Arizona's literary field, that was found by the genius of a lonesome valley's queen, the song-lark of our "Great Southwest."

From the sheltering tree of her ancestral hall shyly she fluttered forth.

Among stony crags of the sierra, on fearsome dizzy trails, in the somber shadows of virgin forests, in the rustling of wind-blown leaves (the seductive swish of elfin skirts) she heard the voices of Juno's sylvan train. Enchanted she listened to the syren's call, and ere the echo died within her ear she had devoted her talent to literature, a priestess self-ordained in Arizona's temple of the muses.

In the flight of her poetic mind she met his majesty, king of the hills, the mountain-lion at the threshold of his lair and toyed with his cubs, princes and heirs to freedom.

She heard the were-wolf scourge of herds, fierce lobos snarl in silent groves of timber and shivered at the coyote's piercing yelps from grave yards in the valleys.

At nighttime, in her lonely camp the dread tarantela disturbed her rest and in day's early gloam a warning rattle of creepy serpents sounded her reveille:

"Fair maid, awake, arise in haste! When darkness vanishes with dawn, heed our alarm-clock in the morn!"

She spoke not to the sullen bear, in cautious silence passed him by and shunned the fetid breath of monster lizards and venom stings of centipedes and scorpions; but woman-like she feared the hydrophobia-skunk more for its scent than for its deadly poison.

She heeded not the half-tamed Indian on the trail; but the insolent leer of Sonora's scum, the brutalized peon, the low caste chulo of Chihuahua, froze into the panic-stare of abject terror under the straight glance of her eye. The slightest motion of her tender hand to him augured a sudden death, for she was of Arizona's daughters, invulnerable in the armor of their self-reliant strength, a shield of lovely innocence, white as the snow is driven.

On the Mesa del Mogollon, in the darkling Coconino Forest she interviewed the cowboy, that valiant belted knight of modern western chivalry, and in the chaparral she cheered the lonesome herder.

In the treasure-vaults of earth, a thousand feet below the surface, invading the domain of Pluto's treacherous gnomes she met the hardiest man in Arizona, the miner, who always happy is and full of hope.

Poor fellows, they hobnob with death and do not mind it!

Floods of rivers, cloudbursts in narrow gorges, the lightning of the hills, blinding and smothering sandstorms on the desert detained her not, for in her chosen path not on delay she thought.

By fragrant orange groves in the valley of Saltriver, past "lowing kine on pastures green," under the luring shade of palms, among the vines she passed.

Winging her virgin-flight to snowclad pinnacles of Parnassus she pours her jubilant songs of hope, faith, love into men's souls and women's hearts.

"May constant happiness attend thee, fair lady, our precious pearl in Arizona's diadem!"

Though time shall wreath thy raven tresses with silvery laurel, and with his palsied hand forever stay, in the fulfilment of thy mortal destiny, the throbbing of thy faithful heart—"Yet shall the genius of thy lyre with angel-hands reverberate the shining chords through untold future ages in heavenly strains of resonance and glory, until the solace of their faintest echoes dies within the last true heart in Arizona."